ISLAND OF BLISS

When Judith booked a holiday in Crete she had not reckoned on meeting Peter again. She had broken off their engagement years ago, putting all ideas of marriage behind her to pursue her career, and had never expected to see him again. Was Fate offering them a second chance? If so, there was one severe complication — Peter had brought Carol on holiday too.

Books by Joanna Gale
in the Linford Romance Library:

CASTLE IN THE SAND

JOANNA GALE

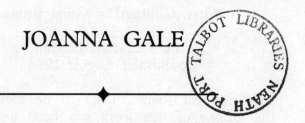

ISLAND OF BLISS

Complete and Unabridged

LINFORD
Leicester

First published in Great Britain

First Linford Edition
published August 1994

The right of Joanna Gale to be identified as
the author of this work has been asserted by
her in accordance with the
Copyright, Designs and Patents Act, 1988

British Library CIP Data

Gale, Joanna
 Island of bliss.—Large print ed.—
Linford romance library
 I. Title II. Series
 823.914 [F]

 ISBN 0–7089–7553–4

Published by
F. A. Thorpe (Publishing) Ltd.
Anstey, Leicestershire

Set by Words & Graphics Ltd.
Anstey, Leicestershire
Printed and bound in Great Britain by
T. J. Press (Padstow) Ltd., Padstow, Cornwall

This book is printed on acid-free paper

1

"DAMN it all — I'm going to be late! The first time I've treated myself to a proper holiday in years and I'm going to miss the blasted plane!"

Judith sat tensed forward in the driving-seat, lips pressed firmly together, a frown of determination between her blue eyes and muttered under her breath, willing the long line of vehicles ahead of her on the M25 either to get a move on or get off. It was all so annoying. She'd allowed hours of extra time to leave her flat neat and tidy, drop her key in to the security-guard and accomplish the short journey to Heathrow. But then the car had taken an age to start. Then there was more traffic about than there would have been had she left when she'd intended. Then every heavy lorry in England

1

had decided to drive, two abreast, just ahead of her, reducing her to a furious bundle of anger and frustration.

She didn't dare scare herself by looking at the time. Just keep driving, she told herself, forcing herself to breathe deeply and managed not to give in to the temptation to hoot loudly and stick out her tongue when a London taxi cut in sharply in front of her, missing her off-side wing by inches. Better to arrive late than dead, she muttered, illogically, to herself. Except, she added grimly, indicating quite savagely that she was going to turn left off the motorway . . . except that she was the sort of well-organised young woman who prided herself on always arriving anywhere unflustered and precisely on time. And today, she vowed, will be no exception.

'Welcome to Heathrow'. The words shone down, unaware of their irritant effect on the purposeful travellers below as they plunged into the tunnel. Judith, hating the fumy atmosphere, stepped on the accelerator, drawing alongside the taxi that had cut her up a minute or two previously and in a childish mood of defiance she stared deliberately into it, to shame the driver into some admission of guilt. As they emerged from the gloom and slowed at the traffic-lights, still beside each other, his gesture was by no means one of apology — and much affronted, Judith turned her head away sharply, her smooth, silky blonde hair whipping round like a curtain to hide the angry blush that had risen into her cheeks.

As the lights changed she could not resist just glancing back at the taxi-windows, vaguely conscious that the passenger, no doubt egged on by the uncouth driver, had been staring at her in an aggressively impudent manner. Determined to maintain her dignity she stared coolly back into that face so close to hers yet so isolated in his separate vehicle — and promptly stalled, her mouth dropping open, leaving herself stranded at the lights while the taxi shot away and impatient holiday-makers behind her hooted and swore as they endeavoured to edge their way past.

Well, of all the . . . after all these years! Annoyed — even a little scared — at finding herself so rattled at being so unexpectedly brought face to face with her past, Judith settled seriously to her driving, the frown between her eyes one of thoughtfulness now. How ridiculous! Why should she be so surprised? Peter — if it had been Peter — was just as entitled to go on holiday or on business as she was. But, if she had known it was him in the taxi then perhaps she wouldn't have behaved towards the driver in quite such a childishly challenging way.

She was almost sure he'd had a girl with him. There had been the impression of the outline of a smooth dark head and pale face beyond his in the back of the taxi. That too was hardly surprising, as Peter had always been an attractive, gregarious, much sought-after man. But the episode bothered her to a quite unreasonable extent and in spite of the fact that she was so late she found her thoughts pre-occupied as she weaved her way to the long-stay car-park, locked up, found a trolley and wended her way towards Terminal Two. She arrived at the check-in desk just as they were taking away the flight-number and had to accept the only seat that was available.

"We'll tell them you're on your way," the check-in girl reassured her, smiling at Judith with calm encouragement and Judith silently blessed her for her pleasant manner and helpfulness. Nevertheless she hastened through all the various stages of passenger-control as fast as officialdom would allow and managed to arrive at the exit-gate just as the last bus to the plane was leaving. She was hauled in by helpful hands.

Suddenly her troubles and responsibilities fell away from her. Surrounded by excited, apprehensive, chattering holiday-makers she felt that first irresistible thrill of pleasure run through her as she gave herself up to a light-hearted holiday mood. Hanging on to the nearest metal pole, hemmed in by family groups, decked out in new clothes and happy smiles, as the bus raced, swaying to the aircraft, she shut her eyes briefly, revelling in the fact that for the next two weeks her life could be totally given up to pleasure and pleasure alone. It was a prospect she felt hardly able to believe.

* * *

Judith lay back in her narrow seat as comfortably as she could, sandwiched between a stout, perspiring man in his fifties and an equally stout Greek matron on the gangway-side. Of all seats on board an aircraft she hated the middle one of three the most. By surreptitious glances at the labels on their hand-luggage she discovered that the uninspiring fattie on her left was on the same holiday as herself causing her spirits to sink just a little, as even after a mere two hours' acquaintance he had proved himself to be churlish, fidgety and none-too-particular about the way he ate his meals.

My fault for being late, she chided herself and closed her eyes, trying to while away the time by dozing. If she'd been sitting by the gangway she could have stretched her legs, had a good look at the other passengers, just . . . well, she could have just checked to see who else was there. Don't be an idiot . . . of course *he* won't be, she continued to lecture herself shifting her arms away as both her stout neighbours claimed the arm-rests as their own. He could have gone anywhere, anywhere in the world and was probably on his way to a conference in New York or a convention in Moscow. Yet, even from the brief glimpse she had got of him, he had seemed too casually dressed for a business-trip. And she had this sneaking feeling that, just as she'd got onto the plane, during those moments of confusion when everyone was trying to settle down, she'd glimpsed the back of his head as he'd pushed some luggage into the rack above the seats miles down the plane; but the moment had been so fleeting that common sense told her that it could have been anyone.

Peter Rowland. Her lips mouthed the name silently as the aircraft flew high above the Mediterranean, the sun pouring in through the small, oval window. Why should she find herself all in a dither at the mere thought of him? Seeing him in the taxi had given her a shock — quite naturally, she supposed. But after ten years apart, having lived an independent, successful life for all that time, why should that one quick glimpse have unsettled her in such a disturbing way? It was ridiculous. She had got Peter out of her system long ago when she was barely nineteen years old.

It was she that had broken their fairy-tale engagement, her decision not to tie herself down to a husband, children and domesticity so early in her life. It had been a hard decision. Her friends and most of her family had thought her utterly mad. Only her mother, even though she had doted on Peter, had understood the reasons for turning her back on security and an enviable life-style and opting for the challenge of her own career and the chance to prove her own worth. The worst part of the whole unhappy business had been her feelings of guilt at having caused Peter such deep unhappiness — after all, she had only been nineteen with years and years of youth still ahead of her, whereas he had seemed so much older to her then — all of twenty-eight years old. She had had to live with the uncomfortable feeling for years after the break-up that she had handled things badly, robbing him of the future he had looked forward to and unwittingly making him look a fool in front of his friends. This was something she was not proud of.

Judith tried — and failed — to stretch her legs and smiled ruefully to herself. Twenty-eight had seemed so mature to her then — now here she was, a whole year older than that herself, with the dreaded three-0 coming up next birthday. Yet she felt not a day older than she had in her teens — wiser, perhaps, more self-assured, certainly more level-headed — but older, not at all. If I'd married Pete I'd have felt older, she mused, imagining herself overweight and distracted, hair in a mess, with two or three children throwing tantrums all around her, worrying her to death with all their petty problems. And Peter — even at his advanced age! — had got over her remarkably quickly.

Even while she was building up her career in office-design, gradually increasing her commissions, thrilled to be working in the increasingly fashion-conscious, colour-conscious world of big business in London she had still followed his fortunes, just casually, as one did with old friends. He had married, just a couple of years after their break-up, a lovely French girl, Yvette, quite beautiful really. She'd seen them together at a smart restaurant near Covent Garden one lunch-time when she had been entertaining a client and had expected as the years went by to hear that the next generation of small Rowlands had arrived. But from what she could gather from mutual friends there could be no babies and quite soon there was no Yvette. Some sort of pernicious cancer, apparently, that had raged through her, reducing her to skin, bone and huge staring eyes in a few short, terrible months.

By the time this had happened Judith was herself in a serious relationship with an unhappily-married man and expected to stay with Steve for ever. Her career was at its most successful, in fact becoming almost too much for her to handle. The thought had crossed

11

her mind — no more than that — when she'd heard of Yvette's death, that now that she, Judith, was older, had proved herself in the world of business and was in a strong financial position, it would have been interesting to meet Peter again, just to see if the old spark was still there. Their paths had not crossed, however, so that was that — and that was more than three years ago.

Since then Steve had gone back to his wife and as for Peter . . . well, he'd be married again by now, she expected. That must have been his wife she'd glimpsed in the taxi beside him. And yet . . . that look he'd given her out of the taxi-window, that lively, delighted, astonished stare had somehow not seemed like that of a married man encountering a long-forgotten, unimportant part of his past. He'd looked older, of course — well, he'd be about thirty-eight by now — but still with that heavenly shock of crisp, wavy, chestnut hair, still those large, rather doleful, brown eyes, that generous, broad smile. And there was no denying that, adoring wife or no adoring wife, he had looked extremely pleased to see her.

* * *

"We will shortly be landing at Heraklion Airport. The local time is three-thirty p.m., the weather hot and sunny with the temperature at twenty-two degrees. Please be sure . . . " but the message about keeping one's seatbelt fastened until the plane had come to a standstill and not leaving one's belongings behind were drowned as a general murmur of approval greeted the news of fine, warm weather. Grey clouds, shiny pavements and the swish of tyres along wet gutters could be forgotten in contemplation of a fortnight of cloudless skies, bright, Cretan sunlight, the smell of suntan-lotion and the buzz of bees busy amongst marjoram and thyme. A rush of scented warmth greeted

13

them as the planeload of pale-faced hopefuls groped their way down the aircraft steps, coats and cardigans flung over arms, carrier-bags already loaded with duty-free booze and cigarettes. Unencumbered by such irrelevancies, Judith strode cheerfully off in the direction of the terminal building, catching glimpses of 'Island of Bliss' labels here and there on the way. But there were several package-tour groups on board and it wasn't until they had passed through Customs and Passport Control and emerged into the Arrivals Hall that the disorganised mass of humanity began to sort itself out. The independent travellers and homecoming Cretans dashed straight off to find taxis, the others craned their necks anxiously all trying to identify 'their' guide.

It took Judith only a few minutes to find Nikos, of Bliss Tours, a slim, handsome Cretan in his mid-twenties. He was holding up his placard, clipboard in hand, pockets bulging with pens, tickets and other paraphernalia, black eyes darting here and there amongst the crowds, after six years in the job able to spot a 'Bliss' label at more than a hundred metres. She smiled coolly at the two young men who had already found Nikos, passing a sympathetic look across their fresh faces, taking in the ear-rings, the well-cut, tinted hair and the fact that they stood intimately close to each other and smelled of a rather delightful perfume; and reckoned she'd have no trouble with either of them. Not that she was looking for trouble, not seriously.

This holiday was intended as a breathing-space, a time for her to get her bearings, to think over and plan the next stage in her life. The last few weeks had been hectic, what with selling up the business, seeing brokers about investing the proceeds and her accountant about tax-matters, to say nothing of taking the cats to kennels and the contents of her fridge to friends in the flat above. She was free . . . for the first time in ten years

15

freedom stretched before her like the yellow-brick road and these Two Weeks of Heaven on the Island of Bliss were intended to be the wonderful start to a new, as yet undecided, way of life.

Her stout neighbour from the flight arrived, huffing and puffing, red-faced and inclined to grumble and agreed, reluctantly, that he was indeed George Green. A family of three then appeared, the woman anxious, untidily pretty and a little too plump, her husband quietly jovial, their daughter . . . an unmitigated disaster. Judith's heart jumped in sympathy as they introduced themselves as Dennis and Rosemary Wallis and their daughter, Brenda, the latter a skinny fifteen-year-old, spotty, sullen, in a childish cotton frock, her hair scraped back from her peaky, bony face. But her eyes, Judith noticed, and her lovely little teeth, were beautiful . . . or could be, given care.

We are seven, she found herself quoting, glancing round the Arrivals Hall, wondering if she were to find herself the only unattached female in the group. Even as she pondered the likelihood of this she saw Nikos's eyes widen and his expression falter momentarily from that of welcome that it was incumbent on him to preserve at all times and in all circumstances as two ladies, well into their seventies, the one large and lumbering, the other skinny, with a limp and a shooting-stick, made a bee-line for them, scattering stray tourists right and left as they approached. The large one, beaming with success, her face beaded with perspiration, gave a great sigh of relief as she gazed round at the little company.

"We're Betty and Margs," she explained, catching her breath, gazing round the airport as if it were a precious ancient monument, "we've saved up for this holiday for . . . how long is it, Margs? Five years. Five years of looking forward to seeing where the Minoans lived and worked and worshipped. And now we're here at last. It's quite unbelievable! I warn you, everybody, I'm going to be the most incredible bore."

They all smiled and laughed except George — and Nikos — and Judith thought she detected something like panic in the young man's eyes as he bent to tick off their names and guessed precisely what he was thinking. This was no ordinary sea, sun and sand bonanza that he was in charge of, but a specialist, activity holiday including a good deal of energetic walking, visiting archaeological sites, museums and 'typical' villages, the whole trip culminating in an exciting, eleven-mile trek through the famous — and sometimes dangerous — Samaria Gorge. The travel-agents were supposed to stress this fact to their customers, hoping to weed out the unfit and unsuitable before they even paid over their deposit. What more could they do? 'This holiday is not for the old and fat' would not look too good in their brochures and would lay them open to all sorts of outraged complaints.

It was not cheap either, the value of the holiday lying in the smallness of the group, which was why Judith had booked this particular one, hating the idea of traipsing round the island's delights with a gang of forty or fifty other people. She found herself surveying the two elderly ladies with a mixture of admiration, trepidation and something else which, after some puzzled reflection, she realised was something akin to shame. Five years those two old dears had saved for this trip — whereas she had decided, almost on a whim, a mere eight weeks ago to splash out on it as a treat and had paid over the money without so much as a second thought. Indeed she'd hardly read a word about the island until last evening. Already, even with three members of the party still missing, their little group had all the makings of a fascinating combination of ages, interests and abilities.

Judith sighed happily, a smile curving

her lips, catching breathless Betty's eye, the older woman's obvious joy and anticipation communicating itself irresistibly to the younger and a thrill of excitement shot through her again. Nothing — and nobody — not grumbling George, sullen Brenda or the two effeminate young men, were going to spoil the next two glorious weeks for her. 'Two Weeks of Heaven' was what the brochure promised — and that was what she was determined to have.

2

ONE should never speak too soon. The first blot on the landscape arrived in the shape of Jeremy Chester, a hearty, sporty type, complete with tennis-racket, ready-made tan and a mouth overfull of bright, white teeth. Judith half expected them to twinkle as he flashed them in a wide grin around the little company that now clustered round Nikos like chicks around the mother-hen. His accent was brashly upper-class, his eyes almost aggressively blue and the lift of his eyebrows as he looked Judith up and down and the suggestion of a wink as he caught her eye set all her automatic defence mechanisms into action. She retreated behind Betty's comforting bulk as the newcomer seemed set on making a move towards her. Her heart sank a little. With two more to arrive, most probably a couple, it looked suspiciously as if she were to be the only single female on the holiday with Jeremy as the only unattached male — apart from George who didn't count — and she instinctively distrusted his flash image and the 'hail-fellow, well-met' sparkle in his eye.

Jeremy's arrival had made their numbers up to ten and Nikos's group was almost complete. He glanced about the various parts of the hall, trying not to let his annoyance show. He knew from experience that if the wait for late-comers was too protracted he tended to lose control of the rest of his party. They would drift off distracted by bookstalls, racks of postcards and souvenir-shops or else they would start to change their money without his assistance — losing him valuable commission. Damn it! Only two more — they must be somewhere! He'd give them two more minutes then go and see if there had been any mix-up over their passports or if they'd managed to attach themselves to another party by mistake. Such things ought to be impossible — and yet they happened all the time.

"What are we waiting for?" demanded Margs, Betty's thin friend, shifting her weight from foot to foot and lifting her shooting-stick as if to prod Nikos with it and fat George chimed in, mumbling to no-one in particular that it was a bloody disgrace and folk had no business to be late and keep everyone else waiting. Judith, more prepared to be tolerant, especially as they were all on holiday and a five or ten-minute wait was surely nothing to worry about nevertheless began to feel the first stirrings of impatience herself. In spite of the warning flashes from Nikos's beady black eyes, she gave into the temptation to wander off a little, just to relieve the boredom of standing still in one place. She stared idly through the airport windows watching the activity on the tarmac. From where she stood she could see straight across to the shop and the Ladies and Gents cloakrooms and gradually became aware of the sounds of a heated argument emanating from that direction. A smartly-dressed, dark-haired, high-heeled woman had just emerged, waving her hands about in the air and was grumbling volubly to a tall, slim man half-hidden from Judith's view behind a Pepsi-stall. The gentleman must have tried to utter some soothing words which only served to irritate his companion still further and Judith heard her reply quite clearly as she snapped back at him.

"God, Peter, it was the most disgusting . . . I mean, it's not going to be like this all the way, is it?" Judith half-turned her head, curiously attracted by the once-familiar name. By this time the irate lady had spotted the group clustered round Nikos who had all guessed that here was their missing couple and she appeared to recoil slightly and remarked, not even dropping her voice, the words easily reaching Judith's ears, " . . . and who on earth are all those God-awful people?"

There was no reply from her gentleman friend who emerged from behind the Pepsi-stall to conduct her towards the group and Judith saw him clearly at last. A hammer-blow of shock hit at her heart! She stood utterly still, transfixed, stupefied. Common sense told her that she had had plenty of warnings that day. That confrontation on the way to the airport, the glimpse of his head in the plane and just now hearing his name. Yet none of these vague reminders of a past infatuation had prepared her for seeing Peter properly again, so tall, so ruggedly handsome, the hair still waywardly wavy. She stared at him, curiously detached, knowing he had not yet seen her, almost stunned with the force of conflicting emotions.

A whole fortnight in his company . . . after what they had been to each other, could she stand it? She ought to dash away now before he had seen her, send a message to Nikos via one of the airport staff, any excuse would do. But the next moment calm and expediency returned. You will not run away, she told herself firmly . . . nor sacrifice the holiday you've paid hundreds of pounds for. She would have to come to terms with the fact that Peter — and his new wife — were to share Two Weeks of Heaven with her whether she liked the idea or not. So taking a deep, determined breath she strolled back with exaggerated calm towards the group, trying to control the ridiculous trembling of her hands. How should she greet Peter? Pretend they were strangers? Greet him like an old friend? Like the too-passionate, too-dominating, too-protective lover that she remembered from the past? Like a former business-colleague? Yes, that would be best. It would be too ridiculous and too difficult a subterfuge to sustain to pretend they had never met.

She slipped back unobtrusively into the group, falling into step well behind

Peter, relieving Margs of the weight of her suitcase, glad of the excuse to have someone to talk to as they emerged into the brightness of sunlight outside the airport. As they waited in the shade while Nikos fetched the minibus, she kept her gaze firmly fixed on Betty's earnest, perspiring countenance.

"We're so anxious to see all the places where the Minoans lived — we're great Arthur Evans fans, you know," she was telling her, "we just can't wait to get to Knossos, we want to see everything, everything . . . oh, Margs, dear, you did remember to pack those books from the library, didn't you?"

There was a warm breath on her neck and the lightest of light touches on her shoulder — and despite the beat of the late afternoon sun, Judith shivered. She made herself turn and look challengingly into his eyes; those same chestnut-brown eyes that had stared into hers with such frank delight from the taxi-window just a few short hours ago. He held out his hand, taking hers in a tight grip. A cautious light smile twitched at the corners of his lips and laughter-lines — deeper and more numerous than she remembered them — appeared at the corners of his eyes.

"So it was you in that saucy green B.M.W.," be said quietly, running his eyes gladly, appreciatively, over her person, forgetting to let go of her hand, "I suppose I should apologise for the driver — not the best-mannered of men, I think." He released her hand and Judith, swallowing hard, noticed how his eyes strayed behind her, looking to see who her travelling companion might be. She anticipated his next question, jumping in before he could ask it, talking rather too quickly, finding herself strangely breathless.

"I'm . . . I'm here on my own. Just sold up my business in London, you see . . . haven't decided what I'm going to branch out into next, so I decided to indulge myself for a couple of weeks. It's the first proper holiday I've had in years." She laughed lightly, looking mischievously up into his serious brown eyes, "I came to get away from it all and . . . !"

"And walked slap bang into your past," he murmured. Then, as if suddenly recollecting himself he turned to introduce the tall, slender, dark girl who was accompanying him.

"I don't think you've met Carol, have you?" Carol shook hands briefly with Judith but her thoughts were obviously distracted, especially as at that moment the minibus arrived, stopping with a screech, showering them all with dust — and everyone surged towards it, treading on each other's toes and bumping each other with their bags.

"We're not going in that thing, are we, darling?" Judith heard Carol utter in disbelief as Nikos leaped out and began heaving suitcases and their owners quickly and efficiently into the bus. He did not appear to boss but somehow managed to make everyone — with one or two exceptions — feel they had just the seat they most desired. There was, fortunately, room for Betty to spread herself across two, grumpy George was teemed with the ever-grinning Jeremy and Judith found herself seated next to the unlovely, but harmless teenager, Brenda. Peter, by accident or design, was seated just across the gangway with Carol beside him by the window. Nikos leaped into the driving-seat and crashing into gear, set off with his last cargo of the season up and around the dusty, Cretan streets.

Heraklion seemed to consist entirely of hills, corners and crossroads, the minibus was old and Betty reeled happily from side to side, clutching at the backs of seats and other people's shoulders and knees. Nikos drove his chariot relentlessly on, dodging lorries, motor-scooters, three-wheeled fruit-carts and taxis with some skill and a good deal of dash and verve. The erratic nature of their journey did not afford much opportunity for intimate conversation but in fits and starts Judith ventured a few remarks. The space between herself and Peter was so narrow it would have seemed churlish to remain silent.

"I'd heard you'd gone to the States," she managed to utter as Nikos was forced, obviously against his will, to slow at a red traffic-light and Peter smiled ruefully and shook his head.

"Wasn't my scene," he replied with a half-laugh of regret and something of a dreamy look entered his eyes, a look Judith did not remember from their time together all those years ago, "nor is London actually, not now. I don't know what's happened to people in the last few years. We used to get super customers in the shop, they became more like friends, really interested in antiques, genuine collectors . . . " He stopped as Nikos swerved to avoid a wayward, trotting horse, pulling a cart-load of scrap, driven, it seemed, by a child of about eleven, " . . . but now all they're interested in is how long

31

before they can expect their purchase to double in value. Very few people nowadays seem to want to buy things for sheer pleasure. There are just a few I shall miss."

"You're off again then?" Judith murmured, bracing herself as she saw the next corner coming up. They shot round it, missing a bus coming the other way by inches. Peter shrugged and shifted a little nearer to the gangway with a half-glance back at Carol who was staring out of the window, her hands tightly gripping the back of the seat in front of her.

"Not . . . not definitely. Just in the planning stage as you might say." He tried dropping his voice which against the roar of the minibus-engine, was not a great success, but Judith was just able to catch the gist of his meaning.

"Trouble is," he seemed to be saying, "Carol's not keen. She's a Londoner born and bred and doing very well with her modelling. What I really want is to give up the retail part of the antiques business and concentrate on advisory and restoration work." He half-laughed and shot a teasing sideways glance at Judith, "Old age must be catching up with me. I've started to dream about doing things we all screamed with laughter about years ago, you know, the communes in the country, eating lentils and letting one's hair grow down to one's shoulders . . . !"

" . . . talking about love and peace, making daisy-chains and walking round in sandals," chimed in Judith and closed her eyes briefly, her shoulders shaking with laughter, "and there we were in the big city, clinching business-deals, making our thousands, driving our expensive cars and thinking they were all completely potty." She looked at Peter in feigned amazement, "Seriously — don't tell me that's what you're going to do?"

"Too right he isn't," cut in Carol who had actually been listening to this conversation without appearing to and she leaned a little across Peter to speak to Judith directly, "It's just a rather annoying bee he's got in his bonnet, one that is going to get well and truly squashed if I have anything to do with it. He doesn't really mean it . . . do you, darling? You see, we've seen this absolutely darling house in Hampstead, Georgian of course, still got all its proper windows and things and plenty of room for a shed in the garden if he insists on messing about with old coffee-tables with woodworm. Strictly as a hobby of course," she added darkly, casting warning glances at him, "I mean, that sort of thing wouldn't even pay the rates. And even with the best will in the world I won't be able to carry on modelling for ever." She leaned even more across Peter, speaking to Judith but really, Judith felt, speaking to him.

"I'm planning to start up a modelling agency in a year or two," she explained, "with my contacts it's the obvious thing to do — so I'm always keeping my eyes open." Judith could tell from

Carol's unimpressed expression that she did not regard her as likely model-material and with a wry smile she leaned back in her seat and half-closed her eyes.

Conversation lapsed, giving Judith a chance to ponder on what seemed to her a strange — almost fateful — coincidence. She and Peter hadn't spoken to each other for ten years, yet she had just sold up her business — very profitably — and here was Peter thinking of selling up his. But then, perhaps it wasn't such a coincidence after all. With so much money floating about in London new businesses were opening up and others closing down or changing hands all the time and curiously nobody she knew ever seemed to lose by it. Many of her friends were in property, making fortunes down in Dockland, leasing or selling extraordinary buildings to young yuppies or go-ahead companies, whilst living themselves in delightful mews cottages in Chelsea or sharing expensively-appointed flats near the Royal Parks. She could easily have done the same. Her old school-friend, Stella, had asked her a dozen times to join her in the estate-agency business and she had been almost tempted once or twice. But she had enjoyed her own work too much, getting a thrill each time she saw a dull, uninspiring workplace blossom under her hands and she was comfortably off, certainly beyond the wildest of wild dreams of a few years ago.

Dusk was approaching as the minibus turned down a narrow side-road and stopped outside the bright lights of a small hotel. It faced directly onto the street, only a degree or two smarter than the ramshackle houses each side of it. As the bags were being unloaded Judith could not resist darting a glance or two at Carol to gauge her opinion of their first night's accommodation, wanting to giggle at the wretchedness of her expression. She must have sensed that eyes were upon her and she swung round, head erect, her dark eyes flashing in her pale, smooth face, meeting Judith's teasing gaze with a malevolent, unsmiling stare. Peter was a few yards away, helping Betty pick up various papers and pamphlets she had dropped in the dusty gutter and, to her surprise, Carol moved up closely to Judith, almost pinning her against the side of the minibus. She took a quick look to check that she was not overheard and thrust her face even closer to Judith's, speaking low through clenched teeth, jerking the words out, almost in a hiss.

"Just . . . just keep clear of him, d'you understand? Just keep out of our way . . . or you'll regret it, I promise you."

Too shocked, too surprised and too angry to think clearly, Judith opened her mouth to reply when Peter reappeared, dusting off his hands and taking Carol, now sweetly smiling, by the arm, the pair of them vanished through the hotel-door, while Judith stared thoughtfully, curiously, after them.

What on earth was happening? She had selected this particular holiday to give herself a period of calm and tranquillity, of time to think and plan her future, a chance to relax and unwind amongst strangers that she would never have to see again. Almost in a daze she entered the little hotel, took her key from Nikos and half stumbled up the stairs to find her room. As she stared through the tiny window onto the busy street below, she reckoned, with gradually stirring excitement that, judging by the shocks and surprises she had encountered during the first few hours on the Island of Bliss, it might be wise totally to revise her expectations.

3

"WHAT a very charming young man."

Judith turned at the words, smiling politely at Rosemary Wallis, Brenda's mother, as they stood in a short queue next morning for the self-service breakfast. She was wondering if she could stomach the strange mixture of slices of cheese, ham and Madeira cake that was on offer. Her eyes slid over the rest of the folk in the queue and the groups already sitting feasting at their tables, wondering which of many equally unprepossessing young men Rosemary could possibly mean.

"That one — that Jeremy Chester," Rosemary said in a hushed, reverential whisper, surprised that Judith had not noticed him, "he's quite a star you know — a millionaire by now, I shouldn't wonder."

"Don't be dumb, Mummy, he wouldn't be on this boring holiday if he was a millionaire." Judith turned with some surprise towards Brenda. These were the first words she had heard the skimpy little teenager utter. She was dressed in a cotton skirt and short-sleeved blouse this morning and if her hair had not been scraped so severely back off her face she would have looked quite presentable in a rather old-fashioned way. Glancing from mother to daughter Judith guessed that Brenda had arrived late in the Wallis's life.

"She wanted to go to Benidorm," apologised her mother, patting stray bits of fluffy hair back into place, "so we've said perhaps next year, haven't we darling? This holiday sounded so exciting with the Samaria Gorge and all, Dennis and I thought, better go now while we're still just about sound in wind and limb. Then," she gave a self-conscious little laugh and Brenda blushed and scowled, "then we find we're not the oldest by a long chalk. I think those two old ladies are really brave, don't you?" Judith nodded, smiling in the direction of Betty and Margs, woollen-socked and sensibly-booted, poring over maps as they drank their coffee . . . and she wisely pretended not to hear Brenda's mumbled "really stupid, you mean." Rosemary had heard, however, and gave her offspring a frosty stare. They all moved on a foot or two and Rosemary tried to balance pots of tea and coffee onto her already loaded tray. Judith offered a spare few inches on hers and Rosemary accepted gratefully.

"Come and sit with us, dear," she said, leaving her no alternative, so she followed them and nodded agreeably to Dennis as she slid onto the chair beside his daughter. Dennis almost blushed as he beheld Judith at such close range and she felt a silent satisfaction that her choice of loose white cotton trousers and a simple, sky-blue T-shirt with a matching bandeau around her hair to stop it falling over her face had been a good one. It was so long since she had been on holiday and so many years since she'd been anywhere near the sea that she'd almost forgotten what one did wear for such occasions. She shot a curious glance over towards the 'charming young man' that Rosemary had pointed out and wondered briefly why, if he were 'quite a star' and (perhaps or perhaps not) a millionaire, she had never before heard his name.

"Tennis," explained Rosemary in a loud stage-whisper and Brenda giggled rudely as her father guiltily jerked his gaze away from Judith's low neckline, looking at his wife in surprised alarm. Betty and Margs had overheard Rosemary and they leaned across, nodding in delighted agreement and Margs uttered in conspiratorial tones.

"We weren't absolutely sure but then brave Betty went and asked him. Oh, yes, it's *the* Jeremy Chester — aren't we honoured! Got into the quarter-finals two years ago, didn't he? Afraid we didn't hear anything of him this year — still, he's young, he's got time."

So that was it — a tennis-star, a rather dim one, Judith surmised and from what she could see at this distance not so very young, not for someone hoping to win Wimbledon. He had good looks . . . that she had to concede, and was tall and hunky, but it looked to her as if his muscles had already begun to revert to unlovely fat. In a few years, thought Judith unkindly as she washed the sweet, dry cake down with a glorious cup of coffee, he'll look like George — and just as she thought of him he arrived for his breakfast, huge belly bulging over his trousers, his face red with the exertion of having got up, dressed and walked down a flight of twelve stairs to the dining-room. What on earth, thought Judith reflectively, as the unpleasant gentleman, not looking to right or left or greeting anyone, made a bee-line for the food . . . what on earth is a character like that doing on a holiday like this? She doubted whether he had come for the culture, seemed so far to have shown no particular liking for the scenery and as for the activities — it looked as if the only activity he was good for was shovelling food into his face as fast as he possibly could.

I'm being uncharitable, she scolded herself — he might be an expert on ancient civilisations, a scuba-diver or even a wildlife fanatic; and though desperately tempted to laugh, did her best to ignore Brenda's none-too-well disguised snorts and grunts as she too noticed the revolting table-manners of their fat friend. She was just thinking that the peaky little teenager might not be quite such a mouse as she appeared when something caught her eye, making her look towards the door just as Peter and Carol walked in.

Carol looked stunning. It simply wasn't fair. How could anyone stand five-foot-nine and look as if she weighed about seven stone? She was wearing trousers too this morning, navy ones teamed with a navy and white striped cotton shirt, a wide navy belt and white leather mules. She looked nautical, willowy, immaculate — and Judith felt instantly self-conscious of her own rather well-developed figure and wished she had worn something more concealing than the bust-hugging T-shirt that Dennis was once more eyeing with obvious delight.

Rosemary noticed where Judith's eyes were straying and, blushing slightly, she attempted the impossible, to attract her attention, to mouth some words of great significance, whilst trying to shield her innocent daughter from some unsavoury truth. Puzzled, Judith leaned nearer, unable to interpret the hand-hidden mouthings and significant looks and eventually Brenda piped up, her thin voice carrying easily from table to table, a look of malicious pleasure in her eyes as she revelled in the embarrassment she caused all round.

"Really, Mummy, I don't care if they

aren't married. This is the nineteen-nineties, you know, nobody gets married nowadays."

A strained silence settled over the room as everywhere folk paused with their cups halfway to their lips, their heads half-turned to try and spot to whom the odious child was referring.

"Really, Brenda . . . " Rosemary was saying, two spots of angry colour blazing in her cheeks; and she began to appeal to Dennis, " . . . can't you do anything with your daughter?" when Carol appeared at their table, arms folded, fixing them all — but particularly Judith — with a malevolent stare.

"I'd be obliged," she said, with icy calm, while cold fury blazed out of her black eyes, "if you'd refrain from discussing my private affairs in public with . . . with children!" She spat out the words and Judith flushed angrily, glancing briefly towards Rosemary to see if she was going to own up to having been the gossipmonger. As it was obvious that she was too overcome to say anything an imp of mischief darted into Judith's brain and she stared coolly back into Carol's beautiful, furious face.

"Whatever made you think we were talking about you?" she uttered, looking as innocently misjudged as she knew how — and she appealed to Brenda, giving her just the slightest wink as she asked her what she thought Carol was talking about. Brenda, quite as ready to tease as she was to revel in scandal, played up rather well, Judith thought, inventing a couple of school-friends who had gone camping together and as Carol stood there, her eyes dark with disbelief her cheeks flushed with the awful realisation that she might just possibly have made a fool of herself Peter came up behind her, not quite *au fait* with the situation, a cheerful smile on his warmly handsome face and greeted everyone at the table in enthusiastic, ringing tones.

"And if you want to dash out for that

bit of shopping, darling," he said to Carol, tapping his watch, "we'd better get a move on. We don't want to get put in the corner by Nikos." His eyes showed surprise as Carol turned swiftly and pushed past him, hurrying out of the room and Rosemary, her cheeks scarlet, tried her best to explain what had happened, darting furious glances at Brenda all the while. Fortunately Peter saw the funny side and laughed, glancing behind him to make sure that Carol was out of earshot.

"Don't worry about it — she's a sensitive girl," he said, pretending to cuff the now subdued Brenda playfully around the ear, "I mean," he added mischievously, his eye alighting as if by accident on Judith, "what does a missing wedding-ring matter between old friends, eh?"

Judith held his glance for a moment or two then looked away, confused, uncomfortable. The others at the table could tell there was some undercurrent, some layer of understanding which they could not share and an uneasy silence smote them all. Peter continued to regard Judith thoughtfully and only turned away, hesitantly, at the sound of Carol's voice calling him to hurry, from the dining-room door.

"Now you see, Brenda," scolded Rosemary, scowling at her errant daughter who glowered truculently back at her, "what trouble you've caused for all of us — and on our very first morning too. Dennis, I do wish you'd speak to your daughter. She's becoming an embarrassment to us both."

"Should've let me go to Benidorm," retorted Brenda and she got up, defiantly swinging her room-key on her little finger, pushing her chair back with a loud scrape. "Anyway," she said as a parting-shot, sending further blushes of shame into Rosemary's hot cheeks, "if he ever does marry that creep, he'll be a right bloody fool!"

"Brenda! Dear!" Rosemary covered her eyes with her hand, unable to bear the shame of having given birth to such a monster, while Dennis and Judith exchanged glances, both of them in severe danger of suffocation as they struggled, for Rosemary's sake, not to laugh.

* * *

Yet, for all the amusement that the episode had afforded them it was a thoughtful Judith that boarded the minibus later that morning, placing herself in a window-seat just behind Mark and Nigel, deliberately as far away from Peter and Carol as possible. Since realising that Peter was to share this holiday her feelings had ranged wildly through shock, pleasure, trepidation and worry, with an underlying sense of foreboding and secret excitement. Carol's antagonism had startled her, upset her in fact more than she cared to admit. But it was understandable. Obviously, in Carol's eyes, she must pose a threat to her present happiness and to her future. Personally — hardly surprisingly — she did not find herself in sympathy with the girl, she seemed hard somehow, selfish and somewhat spoilt — but there was no denying that she was a beauty and if she was Peter's choice then all well and good. She sighed, frowning slightly, wishing she could wipe out the memory of Carol's threats last night and her accusations this morning, wishing also that she, like Betty and Margs could be looking forward to their days excursion with single-minded, untroubled anticipation.

She had hoped that one of the Wallis family would come and fill the empty seat beside her but as luck would have it, Jeremy swung himself up into the bus just in front of them and, fixing Judith with his bold stare, requested the pleasure of sitting beside her. She could think of no real reason to refuse — but wished that Rosemary had not smiled across at them both with such motherly affection as she clambered into the bus and utterly refused to meet Brenda's spitefully gleeful glances as she passed them by.

They had a new driver today, Matthiou, a steady, serious man of about sixty, who — to Judith's relief — drove steadily and carefully, without Nikos's flair certainly, but with caution. While they drove out of Heraklion, taking the smooth, wide National Route towards Gouves and Malia, Nikos set the whole busload laughing, holding up various articles that had been left behind at the hotel, trying to guess at their owners, setting Betty roaring and the bus shaking as he insisted that a tiny, flimsy nightie simply had to be hers. It was almost snatched away from him by a furious Carol and Judith had to endure Jeremy's inane laughter, several none-too-gentle digs in the ribs and his remarks, bordering on the crude, until, to her relief Nikos stood up, a folder of notes in his hand and prepared to lecture his captive audience on the delights in store for them. Half of them would not listen, most of the other half would instantly forget everything he told them . . . but there were usually one or two who appreciated his information which made the effort worthwhile.

He rose, steadied himself against the back of Matthiou's seat, cleared his throat and began.

4

"JUST a few words, my friends, a little background information about the glorious history of Crete before we visit our first Minoan site," Nikos began, deliberately ignoring an unconcealed yawn from George who proceeded to shut his eyes and pull his hat firmly over his eyes. Betty and Margs tut-tutted audibly and a slight ripple of unease flowed through the bus as the scent of possible conflict was detected. Nikos pressed on, directing his words towards Rosemary and Dennis who had kind, bland expressions and looked the endearing sort who would come up to him afterwards with admiration glowing from their eyes and ask him how he managed to remember it all.

"The Minoan civilisation for which Crete is famous reached its peak about 3,000 to 1,400 B.C.," he began, plunging on before either Betty or Margs could challenge him, "the palaces of Knossos, Malia and Phaistos were all constructed between these dates and excavations have shown us the high degree of civilisation that the Minoan people achieved."

"They had flush lavatories, you know," chimed in Betty, thereby ruining the surprise element of one of his prize items of interest that he usually reserved for Knossos, "it says here," she continued, holding her large, black book at arm's length, "water-tanks on the roof would fill with rain and the water was used to flush away the . . . my word, they thought of everything, didn't they?"

"Could do with some of 'em around today," cut in George from under his sun-hat, "my toilet was in a terrible state. 'Ere, Nickers, you write that down. I ain't paying good money fer filthy bogs." Nikos ignored the feeble pun on his name — after six years

55

as a tour-guide he had heard it too often to be either impressed, amused or even indignant and a slight buzz of annoyance issued from the other passengers at the utterances of this most embarrassing man. Looking past Jeremy, Judith noticed Carol wrinkle her nose in sympathetic agreement with George and whisper something in Peter's ear. He slipped an arm comfortingly round her shoulders, giving her a little shake and, suddenly unable to bear looking at them, Judith closed her eyes, leaning her head back and pretended to doze.

Although it was a pity to miss the sight of the golden fields, the pretty whitewashed houses surrounded by verandahs lined with pots of petunias and smothered in climbing plants and the deep-blue line of the sea beyond, she felt quite genuinely exhausted. She had spent a curiously uneasy night, her mind filled with old memories and new speculation. She had often wished, during those frantic, work-filled years in London, that she and Peter had not met when she had been so young. It had been such a thrilling, fulfilling affair, they had been so right for each other, everyone had said so and she'd understood exactly what they had meant. She had been eager, energetic, he had been mature, elegant and clever, already rising high in the world of antiques and the fine arts. In spite of the difference in their ages they had shared the same interests, had ridden in Hyde Park, sailed on the Serpentine, walked endlessly round hidden, little-known corners of London, there had been concerts, exhibitions, the theatre.

They had had dreams of living in a houseboat near Cheyne Walk or in a thatched cottage in the country as all young couples in love like to do and she had been very nearly seduced by the dream. It was only when she had seen friends of her own age who had been at college with her starting interesting jobs, buying their own tiny flats, driving about in their own cars that she realised that she was in danger of disappearing into Peter's life, becoming a mere shadow of him before she had even begun to live herself.

This was where those nine years between them *had* made a difference. He had found his feet in the world, was established, respected, absolutely ready for the responsibility of a wife, children and a settled home, whereas she . . . well, she'd been little more than a child herself. Even when she felt she could not live without him there had always been that slight feeling, almost of panic, when she thought about the finality of marriage, as if to say, "Is this all? Is my life as an individual over already?" Even though it broke both their hearts, she'd *had* to tear herself away to prove to herself that she was a person in her own right. And this she had done, very successfully. But meeting Peter so early in her life had set a standard by which she judged all other men and no-one, not even Steve, had quite matched his style, his warmth and his endearing sense of fun. And now, nearing thirty, she doubted very much whether she would ever meet anyone like him again.

She jerked herself awake, feeling the bus quiver and rattle as Matthiou left the main road and followed the old road down towards the sea and Malia — and looked with interest as Nikos pointed out all the little windmills, sailless now in the late autumn, dotted about the intensely-cultivated fields. The bus crunched up a narrow earth-track and into a stony car-park and Matthiou swung it round, parking beneath an immense olive-tree, facing the sun-washed ruins blazing orange against the dark-green backdrop of wooded hills with above all the deep violet-blue of the sky.

Judith took a ground-plan of the site and walked deliberately alone towards a small gate in the fence, evading Jeremy's inviting looks, steering clear of Peter and Carol, anxious too not to involve herself too deeply with Betty and Margs, the one reading aloud from her book, the other swinging her stick about as she pointed at things in a potentially lethal manner. At least there was no danger of having to listen to George and his grumbles. He'd opted to stay in the bus and they'd left him poring over a huge map of southern Crete, his fat face dripping with sweat, a deep frown between his small eyes.

Judith walked slowly past the series of ruined rooms and granaries, walls and corridors, finding the places, with difficulty, on her plan. Mark and Nigel passed her, meandering along the ancient paved halls as if they were out for a stroll in Regent's Park, laughing amicably together at some private joke. She sat down on a wall for a moment's rest, breathing in the glorious scent of warm herbs, gazing up into the burning sky — and heard the Wallis family pass by, Rosemary telling Brenda how lucky she was to be having such a lovely holiday. The poor kid looked wretchedly hot and irritable and Judith wondered how long it would be before rebellion was once more in the air. She was a plain little thing, no two ways about it — but had a certain individual spirit which Judith was inclined to admire.

She rose and continued down to the vast rectangle of the central court where Nikos, Betty and Margs were holding a learned, archaeological discussion about the stone altar beside the shallow staircase leading to the storerooms. She waved at them but continued alone across the Hall of Columns and made her way to the Hall of the Tower where two giant pithoi stood, immense earthenware jars eight or nine feet tall, the jagged jig-saw pattern of the pieces showing how painstakingly they had been restored. She gazed up at them, shielding her eyes from the glorious sun, sighing in contentment. The warmth, the intimate beauty of the uncrowded site set between the hills and the sea, the far-off voices of her travelling companions and that all-pervading spicy aroma of the Cretan country-side, combined to fill her with an almost choking happiness. She clambered down below one of the pithoi and sat quietly amongst the dry stones of a tumbled wall, revelling in the sunshine, the clear air and the light whisper of the cooling sea-breeze in her hair. Heaven indeed — if the rest of Crete was as sensuously beautiful as this, the brochure had been speaking only the truth.

Suddenly she heard voices from above her, the other side of the huge jar, the one petulant, the other calming, soothing, but with an edge to it that seemed to indicate irritation barely suppressed. Judith froze, embarrassed, unwilling to move from her secluded spot and be discovered, yet hating to overhear other people's squabbles. What should she do? She closed her eyes, hoping they would drift away on their route around the ruins — but they remained, imagining they were safely alone, never thinking to look on the other side of the tumble-down wall.

"Listen, Carol, for God's sake." Judith's heart jumped at the tone of exasperation, well-known to her from times past. Well known, yet rarely heard. She knew from experience that it took a lot of aggravation to make Peter adopt that particular tone of voice. "I'm sorry about your shoes and your blisters and I'm sorry you don't like this holiday but it was you that insisted on coming. I warned you about the walking and climbing, you can't deny it."

"O.K., O.K.," she snapped, but with a catch in her voice that made Judith realise that she was in fact very close to tears, "but what you didn't tell me was that we'd have to be squashed up all day in a stinking bus with a whole load of country bumpkins. God, there isn't one with a scrap of intelligence, they're just a load of frightful morons."

"Carol, that's quite untrue and you're being quite unreasonable," Peter replied but Carol warmed to her subject, convinced she was in the right.

"No, you're unreasonable," she retorted, "why can't we hire a car and travel comfortably? Why can't we go on the beach? I don't want to spend my time wandering about among a lot of old stones."

"Listen," Peter replied swiftly, "we went to Tenerife in the spring because that is what you wanted. Now we're in Crete because it's my time to choose. You didn't have to come. I wouldn't have minded in the slightest coming on holiday on my own."

This observation was greeted by a sarcastic snort and Judith froze, worried in case a stone slipped and belied her presence as Carol flashed back:

"Oh, you'd have liked that, wouldn't you? That would have given you just the chance you wanted to make eyes at that common little tart." With a sick shock Judith realised that Carol was referring to her — and horrified rage swept through her. Peter's voice in reply was tight with fury.

"I've told you, Carol, I had no idea she'd be on this holiday. How could I? I've hardly seen or spoken to her for . . . oh, I don't know, for years, literally years! It's all water under the bridge; Christ, she was only a child! I can't ignore her, can I, one has to be civilised at the very least?" Carol murmured something inaudible and Peter's voice, lower now, gentler, coaxing, replied:

"Listen, Carol, on my honour, as I told you last night, that girl means absolutely nothing to me now. You matter — you know you do — only you." There followed the intimate sounds of sighing and kissing and Judith's cheeks burned with agonising embarrassment. A few minutes later, to her intense relief, she heard their footsteps, his firm and hers stumbling, fade away along the gritty path and, when she dared to raise her head and look after them, they were out of sight.

She rose, guiltily, dusted off her trousers marked with the orange dust that blew into all the nooks and crannies of the rocks and gingerly climbed back over the wall again, gaining the path just as Jeremy chanced to pass by. There was no possible way of avoiding him so she fell into step beside him, answering his questions as politely as she could, hardly hearing his remarks, his compliments. It had given her no pleasure to overhear a lover's tiff. It had marred the peace and beauty of the day. She felt bad about having remained unseen, bad about listening when she could have stuffed her fingers in her ears . . . but what made her feel worst of all, she realised, were Peter's concluding remarks, spoken in earnest to that petulant, disagreeable girl. Jeremy rattled on about tournaments he had played in the States and his planned tour of Australia in the New Year, while all the time those last remarks echoed round and round in her head. " . . . That girl means nothing to me now . . . absolutely nothing to me now . . . "

Well, of course she didn't. How could she expect to? She had given up all claims to him when they had parted ten years ago to take different paths in life. So why did she feel so empty . . . so disappointed . . . so cheated to hear him talk about her as if she mattered less than the dust beneath his feet? Seeing him again had been hard enough to take — hearing him speak so dismissively of her had given her pride a very severe bruising indeed.

* * *

"She's such a good girl, our Brenda — our pride and joy, isn't she, Dennis?" Rosemary's voice overcame the straining of the engine and rattle of the bodywork as the bus battled up the hills around Kavouri on the way to Sitia later in the afternoon. The pretty little town of Aghios Nicholaos, tranquil with its harbour, its boat-filled lake and little bridge, cages of sad, cramped animals and cheerful tourist-shops was behind them. Full of lunch the little company now dozed, sleeping off the effects of Greek beer and rough red retsina or else stared out at the thrilling spectacle of tumbled rocks and lofty cliffs above the bluest imaginable sea. The road snaked away behind them, courageously creeping around mighty overhangs, dipping over bridges, soaring over gigantic bluffs of rock too huge for the road-builders to shift, keeping always within sight of the sea.

The town, visible for miles as a tiny, white smudge between the sea and the hills disappeared at last as the main road forged its way up and down gradients that, from the frequency of small shrines placed alongside the road at the sites of fatal accidents, were hazards to be treated with respect. Judith, not normally a worrier, had on occasions closed her eyes as Matthiou, easing as far out as possible round a corner to clear a rockfall had met a lorry full of sheep, fruit or old motor-tyres thundering towards them in the middle of the road, so she had no idea, apart from the constant squealing of brakes and blaring of horns just how near to death they had all been during the past hour.

Rosemary — having obviously for-gotten Brenda's behaviour at breakfast that morning — was still extolling the virtues of her daughter to kind-hearted Betty, still spread out across her two seats just opposite the spindly child.

"She is certainly a lovely girl," Judith heard her agree with commendable mendacity and Rosemary blushed with pride and drew breath again.

"Never given us a moment's trouble, has she, Dennis? Always such a help around the house. And . . . " here Rosemary intended to repeat her earlier trick and stage-whisper a few words to Betty but the noise of the bus defeated her purpose and Judith noticed the girl cringe as the words — which she must have heard regularly, to her chagrin — came floating down the bus for anyone still awake to hear and to digest.

" . . . and no nonsense, dear, if you know what I mean. I mean, well . . . no trouble with *boys*. We're lucky there, aren't we, Dennis — especially when you read the papers." Betty nodded vaguely and Jeremy, sitting once more beside Judith, murmured, rather too close to her ear for comfort, that he'd have been very surprised if Brenda did find boys a trouble. Even though precisely the same thought had occurred to Judith, loyally she declined to reply, contenting herself with an inward snigger and moved a little away from the window, trying to indicate to Jeremy without actually having to spell it out that he was sitting far too close to her for comfort. He either would not or could not take the hint and, pressing her lips together wearily, she glanced around the bus to see if anyone had noticed how annoying she was finding this rising — or more likely falling — tennis-star's unwanted attentions. Inevitably — she felt — she caught Peter's level gaze as he turned his head away from Carol and she felt her heart jump ridiculously as she noticed how his hair still fell untidily over his brow, almost getting into his eyes.

They had always used to joke about their hair, his so wayward, hers so silky smooth, so shiningly blonde. Her fingers itched and tingled as she remembered as if it were only yesterday the rough feel of that chestnut wavy hair as she'd run her fingers through it, tousling it into a riot of tangled curls, annoying him, loving him ... She blinked hard, drawing herself as far away from Jeremy as possible without actually falling through the minibus window, remembering, remembering ... True — she'd only been a child then, as Peter had remarked to Carol, hardly older than Brenda. Ruffling his hair was just the sort of thing a silly young girl might like to do and he

71

had humoured her silliness for as long as he could bear it, before . . . She shut her eyes tight and clasped her hands tightly together and her breath came in deep, full sighs. Beside her, Jeremy smiled indulgently and leaned against her arm, pleased and relieved to witness — at last — the effect his charm, wit and stunning physique were beginning to have on this enigmatic, unresponsive girl.

5

TO Judith's relief just as she was wondering whether to be explicitly rude to Jeremy, make a scene and demand to change her seat (when in fact there was nowhere else to go) Nikos stood up, clipboard in hand and called his little group to order. George stopped snoring, Mark and Nigel were cut off short in the middle of an argument over who should have paid for last night's beers; Jeremy stopped pressing his leg against Judith's and Brenda stopped writing her name in the dust on the window-pane, turning her rapt attention to the slender young man at the front of the bus, blinking rapidly as he looked round, catching her glance momentarily with his own.

"Well, ladies and gentlemen," he began, trying not to let any doubt creep into his voice as his gaze roved over Betty, studying a map spread over her vast knees and Margs, who had fastened onto her beaky nose a pair of old-fashioned, steel-rimmed spectacles, "we have a trip arranged for this afternoon to the typical Cretan village of Piskekephalo, by foot for about three miles — just to get you all into training for the Samaria Gorge next week. Now then . . . " He bent towards the two old ladies with a look that Judith could tell even from where she was sitting meant, "now, I know you won't be able to make it but I've got to ask you all the same." To his surprise, Betty grasped him by the sleeve, pulling him towards her, nodding vigorously.

"Count us in, Nikos dear, never-say-die, three miles is nothing to us, is it Margs?" Unsmilingly, Margs decided that, arthritis or no arthritis, she and her shooting-stick together could manage and Nikos, having the grace to look slightly abashed, continued down the bus, writing down all the names except Peter and Carol. They wanted to swim, Judith overheard Carol say, leaning across Peter to make her wishes known. Did Nikos know of any well-secluded beaches?

Nikos sat down again with a sigh, scanning his list with some disquiet. This trip wasn't turning out to be the simple, uncomplicated one he'd hoped for to round off the season, what with two old girls to jolly along the rugged path to Pisko, a daft teenage girl making eyes at him already and . . . oh, Lord, he might have guessed, George in full cry, huffing and puffing to no-one in particular.

"What's there to see at this Pis . . . Piskofolous or where-ever it is," he seemed to be demanding, "waste of bloody time, I call it, I've never even heard of the damned place." As no-one, not even Betty, seemed able to supply him with any ready information, Nikos turned again, addressing the red-faced, red-necked, glowering gentleman with as much patience as he could muster.

"It will be a pleasant walk through orchards and olive-groves," he soothed, "nothing too difficult, just a little scrambling over rough ground to get you all into good shape for the Gorge."

"Ha!" broke in George, his eyes suddenly gleaming — and he stole a look around the bus, "that's the place I've come to see — mind yer put me name down for that. Not all the tours include it, yer know, that's the only reason I booked this one." Nikos looked down at the floor of the bus, hardly liking to point out, at this stage of the holiday, that George was hardly the ideal shape, size, age or in the ideal state of fitness to tackle eleven arduous miles over streams, rocks and down steep hillsides. But George was warming to his subject. "It's all booked up, I 'ope, Nickers, I mean, we don't want any cock-ups about the Gorge." To anyone else Nikos would have smiled and made encouraging noises but this overbearing, fat man annoyed him so much, he pursed his lips and frowned.

"Well," he began with some doubt as George's face grew red with furious anticipation, "it is rather late in the season and we cannot run the risk of rain. We never finally decide until the day before at this time of year as we have to be guided by the weather-forecasts. You would not wish to be caught in a flash-flood now would you, Mr Green?"

"Flash flood, my giddy aunt," Judith overheard George mutter and noticed his face darken to an even deeper shade of crimson than before as he turned to harangue the rest of the party. "'ere, d'yer 'ear that? This joker says we might not do Samaria Gorge! Now, look 'ere, Nickers, I booked this trip only because of the Gorge. I don't give a damn fer yer olive-groves or yer Minions or yer fancy flush-bogs." The rest of the passengers, hot with embarrassment, stared at him in disquiet as he continued, "I'll demand my money back if we don't go down the Gorge, that's contrary to my stat . . . statue . . . to my statutory rights, that is . . . and the Trades Descriptions Act an' all." Even from where she sat, three seats away, Judith could feel the heat from the enraged gentleman's breath as he worked himself up into a rage, "If it says Samaria Gorge . . . then we should get Samaria Gorge!" He sounded like a man in a restaurant worried about not getting his free bread-roll and a murmur of criticism started to ripple around the bus. Then Judith heard Peter's voice, clear, uncompromising, cut across the murmuring:

"Time you read the small print, mate," he began, "it's all down there in black and white — if circumstances are beyond our control etc. etc. Anyway," Peter turned full round in his seat to confront the rapidly deflating George, "nobody in their right mind would risk walking down a narrow ravine in the pouring rain."

" . . . nor at any time," broke

in Carol and a ripple of dubious agreement greeted Peter's words of wisdom. Personally, Judith secretly admitted, it would be a severe blow to her if that particular trip had to be cancelled, but, as Nikos was now attempting to explain to them all, if it was not safe to go then he could not possibly allow them to risk their lives.

George fell silent and Nikos took the opportunity, as they were approaching Sitia, to explain before Betty could seize the chance to take over his job, the reason for the sparseness of vegetation and desert-like landscape. Judith listened with only half her attention, her thoughts on George and his unfortunate talent for sowing discord and disharmony.

" . . . as a result of a tremendous volcanic eruption on the island of Santorini in 1500 B.C.," she heard, "and some say that during this period the city of Atlantis was swallowed up by the ocean."

"Fancy that," she heard Rosemary

say, repeating it again for her daughter, while Jeremy took the opportunity almost to brush Judith's ear with his lips as he whispered, "believe that and you'll believe anything," but by this time Judith had stopped listening altogether. From where she was sitting she could see directly into George's seat — he had the odd single one today, beside the sliding-door. As she glanced at him without really intending to, she'd noticed him pull out a handkerchief as if to mop his ever-perspiring brow. But it was his eyes he was mopping furiously turning his head towards the window, sniffling and snuffling, pretending he was only clearing his throat. Much as she disliked the man, her heart jumped momentarily in puzzled sympathy. George — crying! Because he might not go down the Gorge? A grown man? This was extraordinary! There must be something very special down that eleven-mile crack in the cliffs of southern Crete to have such an effect on a person who so far, appeared to have no interest in anything at all apart from grumbling and food. She resolved to buy herself a guide-book, read what she could about it and see if she could solve this rather curious mystery.

Jeremy was digging her none-too-gently in the ribs and everyone — except George and herself — was laughing, Betty roaring and holding her quivering sides.

"What have I missed?" Judith asked, hating to address herself directly to Jeremy, but anxious to know what had caused such general mirth . . . well, not quite general. Rosemary and Dennis were looking doubtfully disapproving, their eyes glistening with protective adoration as they gazed upon their precious, unsullied child while she stared, wide-eyed and open-mouthed at Nikos as he stood before them. Judith's eyes flicked from the handsome head, the flashing brown eyes and slim, neat body to the girl's blotchy, feverish face with something very close to compassion in her eyes, noticing the patches of sweat creeping out from under her arms, the tightness of her clenched hands . . . and half-smiled, forcing her eyes away. Had her doting parents noticed what was happening to their good girl? Couldn't they see that the child who had, hardly surprisingly, had, so far 'no trouble with boys' was about to experience the first adult tragedy of her life by falling in love with somebody who hadn't even noticed she was there? But her thoughts were interrupted again.

"Vai" she heard Jeremy repeat, two or three times, a knowing glint in his eye, "weren't you listening? You must have heard of Vai, the palm beach where everyone bathes in the nude."

"Everyone?" questioned Judith, a startled look of shock in her eyes as she tried to imagine the spectacle that their particular bus-load would present if they all stripped off and exposed their ageing, overweight, wrinkled or otherwise less-than-perfect bodies to the open-air and the gaze of unsuspecting onlookers . . . then wished she had not asked.

"Well," condescended Jeremy, leaning slightly forward in his seat and turning towards her to prevent anyone else participating in their conversation, dropping his voice to a husky whisper, "not everyone. Just . . . well, people like us, for example." He could not help his glance dropping momentarily towards her breasts and his eyes narrowed for a brief, unpleasant second. A wave of revulsion shot through Judith and she folded her arms tightly, staring out of the window. She had had enough of this odious man. Somehow, without spoiling the holiday for everyone else, she was going to have to find a way to put Jeremy Chester very firmly in his place.

During the walk to Piskekephalo Judith attached herself firmly to Betty and Margs, silently blessing Rosemary and Dennis for 'adopting' Jeremy, persuading him (with the greatest of ease) to talk about his past triumphs on the tennis-court and his future ambitions, thrilled to be in the company of such a celebrity. To her surprise, the two old ladies managed the walking without very much trouble. Betty *was* slow and Margs *was* lame but both were made of a mixture of determination and grit that put some of the younger members of the party to shame. Without Peter and Carol to distract her thoughts and revive old feelings, she thoroughly enjoyed the experience of walking through silvery groves of olive-trees, the breeze light and scented, cool enough to encourage exercise, yet deliciously warm as they emerged from the waving trees onto the rocky hilltop, dotted with bee-hives and racks of drying grapes. The village children, bare-footed and mop-haired, all with brilliant black eyes and cheeky smiles, obviously quite accustomed to occasional small parties of intrepid holiday-makers, led them ecstatically around their village, up and down steep, narrow, virtually traffic-free alleyways, the house-walls hung with brilliant bougainvillaea, using their excellent powers of persuasion to encourage them to buy jars of honey, of olive-oil, black olives, green olives, even sprigs of olive-leaves.

"For good luck, Missis," one young entrepreneur insisted on uttering, pressing posies of wild hollyhocks upon the men and women alike, the smile on her face as she received handfuls of small change for her labours, a sight to gladden anyone's heart. Even George, Judith noticed — for she had been keeping half a curious eye on George — had not brushed aside the child as one might have expected, but held on to his posy, rather self-consciously, all the way back over the hillside and through the olive-grove till he reached the bus, placing it, to her surprise, with care on the top of his travel-bag.

"Hoping to take those back home?" she ventured to say to him, feeling that at least someone must try to be nice to him . . . but was rewarded only by a grunt. She was about to carry on down the bus to her seat when to her surprise she found her forearm grasped by George's fat, pudgy hand and she looked down questioningly into his shifty, pig-like little eyes.

"For . . . for me dad," he jerked out in a whisper; then, as if wishing that he had not spoken he abruptly let go of her arm and looked away, scowling, his red cheeks redder than ever after the unaccustomed effort of a three-mile walk, leaving Judith more curious than ever about this unattractive, middle-aged, unpopular and unappealing man. Flowers for his father? Illogically, Judith found it impossible to imagine George even having a father, least of all one who would appreciate the gift of a bunch of dead flowers brought all the way from Crete. She sat herself down by Rosemary — to whom she had had a discreet little chat about Jeremy during the walk and who, bless her, had volunteered her husband to sit beside him on the way home — and between listening to the problems Rosemary had had giving birth to young Brenda she continued to think about George. In spite of his apparent hostility and insensitivity there was more to that strange gentleman than met the eye.

★ ★ ★

The meal that evening, taken alfresco underneath an arching trellis smothered in passion-flowers and dotted with lanterns that swung merrily in the breeze, was excellent; huge steaks of swordfish caught that morning, served with piping-hot french fries and washed down with liberal quantities of retsina. With it came an excellent Greek salad dotted with chunks of feta cheese and luscious black olives, "probably grown in that very same olive-grove we were in this afternoon," as Betty remarked. Carol and Peter had arrived late for supper and although everyone would have been perfectly willing to move up a bit and get the waiter to bring two more chairs they seemed quite content to find a secluded table in a corner and were soon deeply engrossed in an animated conversation of their own. Judith felt slightly uncomfortable as she overheard a few sarcastic murmurings to the effect that "pity we aren't good enough for them," ripple round the table, each sharp remark sparking off a slightly sharper one, fuelled by liberal glasses of the rough red wine, until they were all, with the exception of herself and George, in fits of ridiculous giggles.

"I think . . . we've drunk . . . quite enough," articulated Betty slowly and carefully to Margs, nevertheless accepting another generous glass poured out for her by Nigel, who was sporting a gloriously-embroidered loose cotton shirt. A general 'oooh' went up from the whole table as a platter piled high with exquisite little pancakes, coated with honey and chopped nuts, arrived in the middle of the table. Conscious that she was probably the most sober person present Judith promptly took charge, helping everyone to the sticky delicacies, ignoring all the guilty "well, I shouldn't really . . . " remarks that all females confronted with a particularly delicious dish feel they have to make and she piled their plates high.

Apart from the pointed absence of Peter and Carol it was a lovely atmosphere, with everyone just beginning to get to know each other, all eating and laughing together, their worries and troubles momentarily forgotten. As the meal came to an end, Betty, Margs and the two young men decided to forgo coffee and wandered off, leaving Judith at one end of the table with the Wallises while Jeremy made desultory conversation with George at the other. This seemed to give Rosemary the opportunity, Judith could tell from her expression, that she had been waiting for.

"They make a lovely couple, don't they?" she threw out confidentially, leaving Judith momentarily baffled, unsure whether she meant Betty and Margs, George and Jeremy or even Nigel and Mark. "Those two," she went on nodding towards Peter and Carol, darting little testing glances at Judith, trying in her irritating way — at least it was beginning to irritate Judith — to prevent her daughter from hearing a conversation that might possibly become a little undesirable for innocent ears. Judith raised her eyebrows, shrugging her shoulders — she felt Rosemary's watchful eyes upon her and guessed that there was more to this opening gambit than a mere casual observation. There was a puzzling deep sympathy in Rosemary's eyes as she put out her hand and gave Judith's arm a comforting, though quite unlooked-for pat.

"She's told us all about it," she reassured her in a low voice, nodding solicitously at Judith who gazed at her in some perplexity, while Rosemary continued, unabashed, "and I want to say how *very* sorry I feel for you, my dear — but we can't put the clock back, now can we?" Judith frowned a little, a slight flush of annoyance on her cheeks.

"Who exactly has been telling you what?" she demanded, dropping her voice as she saw an agonised look cross Rosemary's face as she realised, too late, that perhaps she should have kept her sympathy to herself. Brenda, with no qualms about tact or sympathy and who had, of course, been listening all along whilst drawing salt-and-pepper pictures on her table-napkin, looked up, a malicious gleam in her eyes.

"She thinks you're after him again," she supplied, blowing pepper at her mother as she tried to shush her tactless daughter.

"Go to bed, Brenda," snapped Rosemary, turning to Dennis to appeal to him to discipline his daughter . . . and sneezed. But Dennis's chair was empty, his back-view barely visible far away down the street.

"It's like this, dear," continued

Rosemary, hitching her chair a little closer to Judith, "we got talking in the bar after we came back from our walk and they'd come back from the beach. Peter was having a shower and . . . "

"and she was having a pink gin or three," broke in Brenda, her sharp nose twitching at the expectation of some juicy gossip that she knew was on the way. That girl, thought Judith, is going to grow up just like her infuriating mother.

" . . . and we got talking," carried on Rosemary, her eyes darting everywhere to make sure she was not overheard, "and she just happened to mention that you'd once been engaged to her fiancé and that you were just the teeniest bit jealous of her. She said you'd only come on this holiday to spy on them and try to break them up. Of course, I said I didn't think you looked a girl like that and then she told me . . . "

She stopped abruptly as Judith rose, trembling with anger, slamming her coffee-cup down with a bang, hardly able to speak for the fury that was coursing through her. Rosemary looked at her with scared eyes, her hand to her mouth, while Brenda sneezed, scowled, and unaware of the tenseness of the situation said in a perfectly matter-of-fact tone that she thought 'Carol was a cow.'

"I believe you might be right," breathed Judith through clenched teeth — and fighting down the impulse to go over to their table and break a bottle of retsina over Carol's perfect smooth dark hair, she nevertheless swept by the two of them, as close as she dared, glaring into the girl's dark eyes, ignoring Peter's surprised smile and fled up to her room, shutting the door behind her with a crash.

6

JUDITH flung herself onto her bed, her fury at Carol's suggestions and Rosemary's gossip only gradually subsiding. As she grew calmer she scolded herself for her instinctive reaction, her flight from the table, when, if she had only given herself a minute or two to think it would have been so much wiser to face Carol in front of Rosemary and get her to admit the truth. It was all so utterly ridiculous! If she had wanted to renew acquaintance with Peter she could have picked up the phone any time during the last few years or simply walked into his shop in Kensington. Carol must either be very insecure to imagine that an old flame would stalk her lover all the way to Crete or else very vindictive to want to persuade other gullible souls, such as Rosemary, to believe it.

She's clever, too, thought Judith, scowling and snatching at a mosquito that danced just out of reach above her head — choosing someone like Rosemary who couldn't resist the chance of a good old gossip, to 'confide' in. Sooner or later the pathetic little story would reach the ears of the whole group and whatever she, Judith, did or said to deny that she had any such intentions there would always remain some doubts . . . it was only natural. Damn, damn . . . why didn't I take my chance and disappear as soon as I saw the two of them at the airport and before they saw me? Such a stupid situation, so fraught with the dangers of misunderstanding, confrontations, suspicions. Her anonymity was gone, the blessed feeling of being amongst total strangers who knew nothing of one's past besides that which one chose to tell them and, however friendly they were at the time, actually cared nothing for one's future, was shattered into unease and awkwardness.

With how many other people had Carol or Rosemary discussed her past involvement with Peter, sniggering over her supposed ridiculous attempt to win him back? She scowled and sighed heavily and rose slowly from the bed, padding over to the window, opening it and looked down into the busy street below.

There were still a few diners seated round dimly-lit, outdoor tables all along the street, still strollers hand-in-hand sauntering down the very middle of the road, cheerful music wafted up to her ears, mingled with the clink of glasses and sudden guffaws of laughter. The air smelled deliciously of grilled fish, of garlic, spices and herbs and Judith inhaled deeply, even detecting the salty tang of the sea alongside the other rich smells, and a small thrill of excitement shot through her veins. Tomorrow they were going to Vai — a whole day on one of the most beautiful beaches in Europe. Although part of her suggested that it would be prudent for her now to leave the party, to go home before Carol could cause any more trouble, her greater instinct was to stay, defiantly if necessary, to enjoy the holiday she had paid for and prove to everyone that her ridiculous accusations were thoroughly unjustified. Brenda was right — the girl was a cow and, if Judith kept her head and her dignity, it was Carol who would end up looking the fool — not herself.

In spite of this sensible resolution it was many hours before Judith could settle down to sleep that night and not just because of Carol's spite and Rosemary's unwanted sympathy. Visions of Peter kept floating into her head, the Peter she had known before contrasting oddly with the Peter she had met again. At twenty-seven he had been assured, confident, too confident really, had tried to steamroller her into marriage before she had been ready. There was a subtle change in him now however, something very difficult to define and Judith lay, tossing and turning and shaking her head, trying to pinpoint exactly what it was that made him seem different. There was a strange hesitancy in his manner that had not been there before — and he rarely smiled, yes, that could be the difference. The Peter of before had been smiling, laughing and joking all the time, always ready with a witty remark to smooth out a tricky situation. He had been such fun to be with, life had been so simple with him as a solid, reliable rock always lurking in the background.

Perhaps she *had* made an awful mistake all those years ago. But how, she thought, hearing the nearby church-bell strike two, how can one know what is best for oneself at a mere nineteen years old?

It was different now. She felt secure, in charge of her life, quite ready to turn in a new direction, even to be swept off her feet if such a thing were possible at her age, confident that she would land firmly and safely; and could continue alone if necessary. Seeing Peter again had given her a jolt — this was undeniably, deliciously true and in a way it was reassuring to realise that she could still experience that school-girl thrill, that surge of excitement, that almost fearful hope of seeing a certain person round every corner, of hearing one particular voice among the crowd. And as the night wore on towards dawn and sleep gradually overcame her, the frown on her brow was smoothed away to be replaced by the merest suggestion of a smile as memory became a dream — and she was nineteen again.

★ ★ ★

During the night, or early morning, a resolution had formed in Judith's mind, if it was humanly possible, not to look at or try to speak to Peter again, in order to give Carol no cause for worry, Rosemary no cause for speculation — and herself no excuse for idle dreams. So it was with something of a shock — she could hardly tell whether it was pleasant or unpleasant — that she noticed that Peter entered the minibus alone the next morning, flopping into his seat and closing his eyes with the air of a man who had just gone through a trying experience. For once, Judith was glad of Rosemary's nose for information, whispered loudly to Betty and Margs who were sitting just behind herself.

"Too much sun yesterday — she was sick all night and has got to stay indoors today." Not only was Judith perfectly able to hear this confidence but Peter also as he opened his eyes, turning round in his seat, addressing the three ladies and anyone else who cared to listen.

"Yes, poor old love, she's looking a bit . . . well, blotchy and runny-eyed at the moment. And before you all jump to the conclusion that I'm a heartless beast, leaving her to suffer alone . . . " Rosemary had the grace to look shame-faced and Judith stifled a smile, " . . . let me tell you that she practically threw me out. It'll do her good to have a completely restful day in the cool — she should be OK by the evening."

"Worse luck," Brenda was heard to utter before her mother could stop her and Judith looked out of the window, seeing nothing of the scenery as they drove the few miles to Vai, scolding Fate for making her new resolution so difficult to adhere to, but determined nonetheless to behave with the utmost propriety for the entire course of the day.

Nikos stood up and uttered his usual warnings about sunburn and sunstroke, sold a few cotton sunhats which he always prudently brought with him on this particular trip and distributed packed lunches to the members of his party, offering with a roguish grin to rub all the ladies' backs with sun-cream on request.

"Not if I get to them first," Judith heard Jeremy say, giving her a wink from the other side of the bus and she made her second resolution for the day, silently chuckling at the difficulties that might lie ahead in trying to avoid the attentions of two such very different gentlemen. She found herself wishing either that Brenda were a little older and more curvaceous or that Betty and Margs were about half a century younger and (in Betty's case, anyway) slightly less so. With Carol indisposed, there were definite disadvantages to being the only reasonably-shaped and youthful female in the group — as even George had begun to cast speculative glances in her direction.

An hour later Judith lay full in the sun, the gentle echoing tinkle of bells breaking in most pleasantly upon her thoughts. The sea smacked gently at her feet, conversation and laughter came and went in overlapping waves and the sun burned redly through her closed lids. She was enveloped in sunshine, wrapped round in warmth, her whole body drenched in sea-air and drowsy heat and her thoughts — like last night — were lazy dreams. The petulant baa-ing of sheep or goats mingled with the jingling bells and she roused herself, curious to know what could attract such animals down to the beach. Behind the strand ran a freshwater river which widened into a fair-sized lake and then she saw them, a herd of some sixty goats, shaggy-haired, black, brown and dirty-white, plodding through the sticky mud, searching for the clearest pools, their heads raised from time to time as the bleating calls rang out.

The shepherd sat on the wooden bridge that crossed the river in one joyful leap, his bare legs dangling over the edge, his stick tapping and eyes roving over both the herd in his care and the feast of naked human flesh that sported itself before his saucy Greek eyes. Judith felt overdressed in her brief bikini as she glanced around, amazed to see how the beach had filled since their own arrival, with whole groups of youths and girls decked in nothing but their golden skins lazing on the sand or splashing in and out of the sparkling water. After the first shock of seeing so many naked bodies on display, there was nothing to upset even the most prudish maiden aunt as there seemed an unspoken code amongst these happy-go-lucky children of nature that forebade any embarrassing intimacy while other people were about.

"Aren't they sweet?" she heard Betty say as she heaved her huge, wobbly body more upright against the rocks, "just like a lot of children running about with nothing on and enjoying themselves." She looked distinctly envious and Judith held her breath, wondering when to expect Betty's huge, flowery swimsuit, which looked as if it had been made for a three-piece suite, to be peeled off and flung away. She had deliberately attached herself to the two old ladies again, sitting beside them for her picnic-lunch and had felt childishly useful handing out paper-plates, pouring iced drinks, dividing up the bunches of grapes into manageable sizes.

She could not remember performing any such little acts of service for anyone for weeks, if not months — and it made an agreeable change. The men, Peter, Jeremy, George, Mark and Nigel had made a camp for themselves about thirty yards away amongst a semicircle of palm-trees and at first had played all the usual silly games, beach-football and beach-cricket on the smooth sand, until the naked youngsters had arrived. The Wallises sat together, somewhat primly, mother and father protectively each side of Brenda between the two groups. Rosemary looked the picture of gloom as the beach filled up and Judith had almost had to drag Brenda up by the arms before her mother would allow her to run down to the sea, past several somnolent couples, for a quick splash and a swim.

Poor Brenda, Judith thought, remembering the thin bony body and pale peaky face, made to seem even thinner and peakier by contrast with the healthy, glowing bodies all around — today was certainly an eye-opener for her! She sat up and re-packed the picnic-bag, brushing a few crumbs from where they had lodged on her sun-creamed skin and stood up, stretching her limbs. Betty grunted and heaved about, trying to get comfortable on the sand and Margs, dressed in a cotton frock, her legs encased in stockings and with a large, shady hat on top of her small head, let her eyelids close completely as they had been trying to do for the last half-hour or so.

"I'm off for a swim," Judith murmured to Betty, leaving the large lady her towel to drape round herself like a shawl — her shoulders were already turning a rich shade of pink, "over to the island. Don't worry about me, I'm a strong swimmer and I may do a little sunbathing once I'm there."

Betty grunted again and Judith left the two ladies snoozing and stepped down to the waves, dipping her toes in the water, gasping at the cool shock that chased up her body, turning her face up to the sun, shaking her head and letting the light breeze blow freely through her hair.

She was thankful she hadn't turned tail and run off back to England. This was quite utterly wonderful. She smiled, bending down to the water and splashed herself all over like a child in the bath, wanting to turn and laugh and dance and invite the world to come into the water and splash with her! She walked out to sea, plunging deep, exulting in the fresh flow of water about her limbs and the cool, green world that wrapped her round. She floated, eyes shut against the sun, then began to swim with slow, strong strokes towards the little rocky island that lay about a hundred yards off-shore, feeling herself deliciously alone in the world. Tears of sheer joy ran down her cheeks and mingled with the gentle, slapping waves.

The island was deserted when she

heaved herself out onto a smooth, jutting rock a few minutes later. Everyone else seemed to be back on the beach, eating a late lunch or taking a siesta after an early one and she picked her way carefully over the pitted rocks to the side of the island facing away from the beach where the rocks sloped more gently down to the water making a tiny beach of its own. She stood up and looked all around. Apart from two white sails miles away on the horizon and the thin whine of a jet-plane as it passed at 30,000 feet above her head, she was totally alone. After a final glance back at the beach and the empty stretch of sea between the island and the shore she lowered herself onto the flat rock beside the sea and quickly rolled her costume off, placing it on a dry rock well within her reach and slowly lay back, letting the sun fall fully onto her newly-exposed skin, smiling as the heat seemed to bore right through her, soaking into every pore and filling her with warmth and health. She slid into the sea for a glorious, sensual minute, laughing at the sky; then climbed out and sat on a rock, leaning back on her hands, one knee raised and half-closed her eyes. Whatever happened on the holiday now or whatever happened in her life she had these moments of solitary bliss to remember — and she turned her head this way and that, worshipping the sun.

In spite of the sheer, outrageous joy of sitting naked on an island in the Mediterranean, it had to be admitted that hard rock on bare skin was not particularly comfortable. She gathered up the blue, striped cotton briefs and slipped them back on, then tiptoed down to the sea again. As she stood there, watching the sailing-boats race each other across the deep turquoise water, she was suddenly aware of a light vibration through the rocks that had not been there before — and a leap of fear clutched suddenly at her stomach. An earthquake? Would she be swallowed up, sunk without trace like Atlantis, her disappearance along with the tiny island one of life's mysteries to be turned into legend, told and re-told to generations of sun-worshippers to the end of time? The next instant she recognised the vibrations for what they were and relief — and a new disquiet — entered her mind. Someone coming! What should she do? If it were one of the naked couples she would look foolish to be caught hastily donning the top half of her bikini. But suppose it were . . . well, Jeremy — or even George! It was one thing to offer up one's body to the wide sky and the sun, even to be seen by strangers in the same state of nature — quite another to be leered at by fellow-tourists whom she would have to face at supper and breakfast every day for the rest of the fortnight.

She sat down and reached out her hand towards the bikini-top. If it was someone unpleasant she could always grab it, slide into the water quickly, swim round the island and back towards the beach. But as she half-turned to see who had dared to disturb her peace and invade her privacy she remained, still as a statue, her heart lurching uncomfortably, her throat closed up with a sudden choking, inexplicable emotion, as her blue eyes met the gaze, steady and strangely shy, of the very man who had figured so uncomfortably intimately in her recent dreams.

"Peter," she said, her voice low, unable even to affect an air of cheerful disregard — and she let her hand drop from her bikini-top. Peter picked it up instead, holding it up, regarding it quizzically as if it was something he had just fished out of the sea and offered it to her with his broad, warm smile.

"Were you thinking of putting this thing on?" he asked, managing to keep his eyes firmly on her face and Judith, recovering slightly, shrugged and pursed her lips. Did it really matter? With

Peter? It seemed ridiculous to put it on now anyway just when she was beginning to enjoy herself.

"It's OK. Seems to be the fashion around here anyway," she murmured, scooping up a handful of water and letting it run deliciously over her knees.

"Not half," she heard him reply and then came that chuckle she remembered; deep and throaty as the lines around his eyes deepened agreeably. He sat beside her, tossing his hair back with one hand and once more that stab of sweet memory shot through her — and she closed her eyes, looking deliberately away. This wasn't fair — she had tried to avoid him, really she had.

"Sorry about Carol's . . . Carol's indisposition," she murmured, in an effort to keep the conversation light and casual, conscious that Peter was unashamedly looking at her now, his eyes roving over her in a way that made her skin prickle until she wanted to scream. Again came that half-chuckle and a sideways, teasing glance.

"I'm quite sure you're not, my dear," he replied; and as Judith muttered a protest he waved the words away, "It's all right, you know, you don't have to be polite about Carol. She hasn't been exactly polite about you."

Judith smiled grimly, her lips thin, her hand trailing in the water.

"It can't have been much fun for her suddenly to discover that one of your . . . your old girl-friends was on the same holiday," she said, amazing herself with her own sweetness and charity, "It was probably a simple defence-mechanism that made her tell Rosemary I'd chased you both here." Peter stopped splashing the water with his toes and turned to her, his eyes troubled and his forehead deeply creased before replying:

"Is that what she's been saying? Oh, Christ." He turned away, his lips thin, unhappy, "It's . . . it's really not her fault, you know, Julu, she's . . . well, ultra-sensitive I suppose, in more ways than one. She's terribly afraid of losing me after . . . well, after a bad experience with her last boy-friend. I won't bore you with the details — but he did let her down rather badly."

Pity you had to be around at the time to pick up the pieces, thought Judith, wanting to say all sorts of things, wanting to warn him about marrying someone for pity's sake, about being made use of by a disappointed woman, about . . . oh, about a hundred and one things that she could never, never actually say. After all he was a grown man. He should not need warnings or advice about women at his age.

They talked a while, not really looking at each other, filling in details of the past ten years, laughing at the coincidence that had brought them together again.

"Who'd have thought," Peter said as she splashed cool water over both their burning bodies, "all those years ago, when you gave me the heave-ho, that one day we'd find ourselves alone on a Greek island in the middle of the Mediterranean with . . . " he allowed his gaze to drop briefly onto her full, pale breasts, the skin slightly flushed with tender pink from the unaccustomed exposure to the sun — and Judith clenched her hands tightly on the rocks beside her, so conscious of the nearness of his hard, lean body it was all she could do to stop herself toppling over into the sea. His voice was husky as he managed to continue, " . . . with practically nothing on. Oh, Julu, you can't think . . . you can't think what . . . "

All of a sudden his voice tailed away and his head drooped towards her and in a sudden rush of crazy feeling she cradled him against her nakedness for a glorious few seconds, feeling the roughness of his cheek and springiness of his hair against the softness of her skin as they rocked together to and fro, filled with glorious sunny, summer madness. Eventually he raised his head, his glowing brown eyes mazed, unfocused, his hands fumbling to pull her face towards his. They kissed, a long, slow, stolen kiss, one they both knew they should not have, pressing their lips and bodies together as if trying to merge into a single, indivisible form until, breathless, they broke away gasping and Peter turned a little away from her, holding his face in his hands. They were both silent, slightly stunned by their own actions, unsure whether to rejoice or weep.

After a few seconds Judith quietly slipped on the top half of her bikini and with an anxious glance upwards at the sun, still blazing mercilessly out of the sky she took a step or two into the sea. Peter raised his head, looking at her for a long moment then slowly stood up and walked towards her through the water, gripping both her hands in his, his lips grim — and he shook his head as if in anger and reproof.

"I'm sorry, Judith," he said as they dropped hands and turned to swim back across the sea towards the beach, "that was all my fault. I can't deny I enjoyed it . . . my God, I enjoyed it . . . but the fact remains, it was an absolutely bloody stupid thing to do."

7

PETER and Judith swam back towards the beach slowly, each busy with their own disturbing thoughts. A few yards from the shore they encountered Mark and Nigel who splashed them playfully, enticing them to join in a little mild horseplay among the waves and the tension between the two of them gradually eased. As she picked her way across the burning sand to reach Betty and Margs, Judith noticed how Rosemary — and Brenda — followed her, the one accusingly, the other gleefully, with their eyes and even Betty, emerging from her slumbers could not resist treating her to a saucy wink as she settled herself beside her again.

"Good swim?" was all she said however and Judith sighed, nodding happily, closing her eyes in momentary delight. Dennis, Rosemary and Brenda began to pack up and head towards the café at the far end of the beach, Rosemary murmuring something about getting a nice cup of tea.

"Glorious — this island is just glorious," Judith replied and tried not to track with her eyes the path across the sand that Peter had taken on his way back to his pile of belongings amongst the palm-trees — to no avail. Despite herself she turned her head slowly, watching him lightly towel himself dry, slip on a shirt then lower himself gradually onto a blanket, lying on his stomach in the dappled shade, one arm curved protectively about his head, the other flung out carelessly amongst the rocks. Even from a distance of thirty yards she noticed how the springy hairs along his arm blazed redly in the sun and looked away, feeling slightly sick. She plunged her fingers into the sand, lifting up handfuls of the hot, silky grains, letting them run through her fingers again and again, until a series of tiny pyramids surrounded her feet and legs. Her body burned, not just with the effect of so much unaccustomed sunshine but with a hopeless, almost overwhelming desire to race over to him, to fling herself on the blanket beside him and crush that brown, outflung hand hard, hard against her body. Their moment of madness on the island had awakened hopeless, ridiculous longings in her, sabotaging all her wise resolutions to regard him merely as an old business-acquaintance, a cast-off.

Their kiss, their brief contact had been utter magic, unlike anything she had ever known, more sensual, exciting and exquisite even than those long, slow kisses and hours of teasing, innocent love-making they had enjoyed in years gone by. Why, she pondered fiercely, turning her back towards Peter, deliberately facing Margs, fast asleep under her shady hat, mouth slightly open, her book on Knossos half-buried in sand? What was different now? Was it because he belonged to someone else? Because it had been a stolen moment, more precious because it should never have happened? Was it . . . and here Judith frowned, her lips trembling with anxiety and annoyance, crashing all the little pyramids down one by one with her hand . . . was it because, against her will and most certainly against her better judgement she was beginning to see him again as she had when she was a young girl, beginning — she hardly dared to let the thought enter her mind — beginning perhaps to fall in love with him all over again?

I'll be an idiot if I do, she said to herself, and sat up, clasping her knees, gazing moodily out to sea, shielding her face as Mark and Nigel chased each other across the sand passing rather too closely in front of her. An idiot to fall for him when he has that sylph-like, super model-girl in tow. But she'll make him unhappy, was her next thought — and would have worked herself up into a fine state of melancholy and confusion had not Betty suddenly decided it was time she moved and started to gather up her belongings. Her squeals of discomfort when she realised she had allowed too much sun to strike her puffy, pale flesh jerked Judith out of her day-dreams and she and Margs fussed round Betty, bringing water from the sea to cool her flushed skin, helping her ease her vast cotton skirt and blouse (both really far too tight) over her ample, suffering body. By the time they had got her dressed it was almost time to rejoin Nikos and Matthiou in the minibus so gradually everybody regretfully heaved themselves up and said farewell to the sparkling sea. Betty's arms and legs were as bright as newly-boiled lobsters.

"I shan't forget Vai in a hurry," she muttered in Judith's ear as they shuffled their way through the hot sand back to the car-park by the café where they spotted the Wallis family eating chips with one hand and waving off clouds of flies with the other — and stopped a moment to get her breath, glancing at Judith with surprisingly penetrating eyes, "and neither will you, my dear, will you?"

Judith did not reply but merely shivered a little in spite of the heat. Was it that obvious? She knew she blushed as she met Betty's sympathetic, slightly reproving gaze and looked away, confused, irritated by Betty's perception and her own reaction. She compressed her lips firmly as they all found their seats again on the bus, clasping her hands determinedly together. To avoid any unpleasant confrontation with Carol and to prevent the situation getting out of hand she must, from now on, remain constantly on her guard.

★ ★ ★

It was obvious next morning that Betty had spent a wretchedly uncomfortable night. Her poor face was puce and her shoulders covered in long, yellow blisters. Her usual hearty chatter was silenced when they met together at breakfast and Margs nagged her quietly but constantly throughout the meal. Judith regarded her with genuine concern, worried for her . . . and sat beside her to drink her coffee. Betty sat before a totally empty plate, her head hung in misery and shame.

"I'm being such an awful nuisance," she confided to Judith when Margs left the table to fetch herself another glass of fruit-juice, "and it's all my own stupid fault. Everyone warned me not to sunbathe for too long. I'm just a silly old woman and I've gone and spoilt the holiday that Margs and I had saved up for and looked forward to for years." Two fat tears welled out of Betty's puffed and swollen eyes, rolled down her pink cheeks and plopped onto her plate. Judith, not daring to pat her shoulder, arm or knee as she felt instinctively inclined to do, swallowed hard, staring in sympathy as once more the old lady winced in pain.

"It's my bust-bodice," she confessed, "the straps, you know," and Judith narrowed her eyes in thought.

"Listen," she said, "when we get back to Heraklion later today why don't we get you togged up with a couple of those gorgeous, embroidered, loose cotton tops, then you won't need to wear a bra. And I promise you'll feel better in a day or two, so long as you keep out of the sun and give your skin a chance to recover," Betty looked up at her gratefully and tried to smile, "and now," went on Judith, "we can't have you starving. I'm going to have some yoghurt and honey and I'll fetch you some too."

Betty nodded obediently, surreptitiously drying her tears and Judith joined the breakfast queue just ahead of Carol who, though still slightly flushed, looked completely recovered from her overdose of sun the day before.

"It's Betty in a bad way today," Judith volunteered, feeling it was too

125

childish for them to stand next to each other in total silence, "the midday sun can be really treacherous, can't it?"

"Not only the sun," was Carol's barbed reply, treating Judith to a hard, meaningful stare. Judith tensed and frowned — had Rosemary been at work again, she wondered, spreading rumours, stirring up the sort of trouble she seemed to revel in? Curiosity got the better of Carol eventually and she turned to look towards Betty, an expression of revulsion crossing her face as she saw the state the old lady was in.

"God . . . that's really disgusting," she uttered in the tone of voice that suggested that Betty had no business to mix with decent people such as herself — and Judith could see from the self-conscious jerk of her shoulders that Betty had heard this remark. Not trusting herself to speak she went up to the breakfast-table, sliding two bowls of thick, creamy yoghurt laced with dark-golden honey onto her tray and turned sharply to head back towards her table, just as Carol, her attention still on the hapless Betty, turned to help herself to coffee and toast. They collided with a crash, the yoghurt and honey splashing all over Carol's loose, silky cotton dress, dripping in a white and yellow stream down the expensive pink material inexorably towards her legs and shoes. There was a split-second of horrified silence as the two girls stared into each other's eyes — then, just as Judith opened her mouth to apologise, Carol's hand came stinging sharply across her face. Her expression was one of venomous hatred. Two waiters instantly appeared, trying to clear up the mess, but when one of them started to dab ineffectually at her dress with a sopping-wet cloth Carol tried to stamp her foot — which by now had become stuck with honey to the floor — and began hysterically to screech abuse at them, at Judith, at Dennis and Mark who had jumped up to try to offer assistance, finally at

Peter who, coming into the dining-room after a brisk morning walk to buy an English newspaper, arrived to find chaos and confusion everywhere and almost everyone in tears — of either distress or helpless laughter — as the scene took on more and more characteristics of a music-hall farce with every moment that passed.

"It's ruined — she did it on purpose — *she* did it!"

"She just . . . just threw it all over me! I'll sue you . . . I'll bloody well sue you!" Again she tried to step menacingly towards Judith who still stood, her hand against her cheek, open-mouthed with mingled outrage and shock — but with her feet fast on the floor, Carol merely stumbled awkwardly against the table. The temporary silence that this utterance wrought in the room was shattered by the sound of Brenda's high-pitched giggles, which stopped abruptly as Carol swung round — and the youngster ducked, thinking she was going to throw something at her. By this time Peter had reached them both and after glancing furiously at Judith, he surveyed the dripping, sticky mess that was once Carol, shoo-ing the waiters away, looking her up and down, concern and perplexity showing in his face.

"I . . . I'm most dreadfully sorry," began Judith, finding her voice at last, "but honestly, it was a complete acci . . . " but before she could finish Peter swung round on her, pushing her quite roughly out of the way.

"I think you've done quite enough," he said, a deep frown changing the whole expression of his face from solicitude to severe displeasure, "I'm getting bloody fed up with the way Carol keeps getting upset. If it was an accident how come it's only Carol that's covered in yoghurt and not you too." Disregarding Judith's blurted explanations he turned again to Carol, fury rendering her speechless, her whole body shaking with distress and anger.

"How the hell are we going to

deal with this?" he said, glancing from the ruined dress to the ruined shoes and back to Carol's mutinous face. Helpful suggestions came flooding in from various parts of the room.

"She could always take her dress off." suggested Jeremy, with a grin that was almost a leer and stepped forward as if to offer his assistance, but Carol struck out at him with a sticky hand and he retreated. Judith, who had taken a shocked step or two back after Peter's unjust reproaches, ventured forward again, careful to avoid the sticky floor.

"That's actually not a bad idea," she said, trying to do her bit to mend matters, "step out of your shoes and dress then you won't drip everywhere and make things worse. Have you got a bathrobe or anything I could bring you?" At the sound of Judith's voice Carol shut her eyes and boxed at the air with clenched fists. Peter turned again and, placing his hands on her shoulders, pushed her, none-too-gently, back to her seat beside Betty.

"Can't you see," he uttered between clenched teeth, "that it's you that is making things worse?" His breath came in deep, hard gasps and his face held an expression of fury that made Judith fall silent, fearful of his changed mood, "Just keep out of this," he continued, "you've done enough damage for one day." Carol had managed by now to extricate herself from her shoes and with the help of the hotel-manager's wife had somehow gathered up the skirt of her dress into a bundle. But Peter had not finished with her or with Judith and he stormed on, oblivious of the ranks of curious holiday-makers who had all stopped eating their breakfasts the better to enjoy this free episode of high drama.

"I'm just about at the end of my patience with the pair of you ... I mean it, both of you. Behaving like a pair of gutter-girls!"

Judith had had enough. She rose sharply, knocking Margs' stick off her chair as she went and with one furious glance at Peter she left the room, holding her smarting face arrogantly high. As she passed their table she caught Brenda's eye, noticing her spiteful smile and momentarily hated the child for her obvious malicious delight in the situation. Oh God . . . this whole holiday was turning out to be a disaster! After yesterday too, that glorious day! How could one split-second of time, one small accident so completely change the atmosphere from one of cheerful fun to one of simmering tension? How could she face all those people again after being publicly slapped by Carol and humiliated by Peter? It was all so . . . so bloody unfair! Whatever they might think she had done she had quite honestly not meant to do anyone any harm.

Judith hated crying and had trained herself from the age of about fifteen never to give in to the temptation to do so. But now as she sat at her mirror gazing at the four bright red lines that showed up clearly on her face she fell prey to great swamping waves of misery and self-pity, seeing again the venom in Carol's expression and hearing the rough note of accusation in Peter's voice.

"Damn and blast them both," she uttered sternly to her reflection, "they don't matter and I'm not going to let them spoil my holiday." But it was spoiled — temporarily at least — thoroughly and completely ruined, her calm shattered and her carefree enjoyment fled. As she began slowly to re-apply her make-up, trying to cover up the marks of Carol's slap, she found suddenly she could not see clearly what she was doing. The outline of her face became blurred and her eyes felt uncomfortably hot. Before she realised precisely what was happening she held her face in her trembling hands — and cried and cried.

★ ★ ★

Nikos was puzzled. This group — no different as far as he could tell from all the other groups he had led round Crete that summer and many other summers — was acting most strangely as the days wore on. Usually by the fourth or fifth day as they re-entered Heraklion before venturing towards the western end of the island the individual members of the party had become a unit, as if the heat of the sun at Vai had melted them together to become a manageable whole. Camaraderie tended to replace cautious friendship, little groups of like-minded people would form, one or two couples emerge — and, most important of all, his own position as leader was by now usually tactfully but firmly established. None of these expected events seemed to be happening this time, in fact the group seemed to be splitting apart and an atmosphere of unease, even of antagonism seemed to pervade the minibus as the occupants sat silent and subdued as they drove back towards the capital city. What was wrong with everybody? Betty he knew was in pain and unhappy and he'd had to rush about buying her preparations from the pharmacy. Her friend was self-righteously disapproving and seemed to be blaming him for her condition. The Wallises seemed still to be in a state of shock after their experiences on the beach at Vai, George was still obsessed with his worries over whether or not he'd see the Samaria Gorge, while Jeremy seemed generally discontented, no doubt suffering from his notable lack of success in sweeping at least one girl off her feet.

The handsome couple, Peter and Carol had had expressions like thunder on their faces ever since they got on the bus and as for Judith . . . Nikos glanced in the mirror to try to spot her sitting near the back of the bus — she of all his group looked least of all as if she were enjoying her holiday. The only people who seemed at all carefree — as Nikos liked them to be — were Mark and Nigel. And to add to his problems it looked as if that skinny little scrap with the watchful eyes had conceived a hopeless passion for him! Whatever he did and wherever he went he was conscious of those parted lips, that air of attention and those eyes relentlessly following his every move.

He sighed and stood up, determinedly jaunty, ready to give out the details of the itinerary of their next three days in Heraklion. But his forced brightness and too-wide smile were lost on almost everyone, sunk as they were in their own particular melancholy thoughts and to his chagrin it was only the faithful Brenda who appeared to appreciate his information. He sat down again, a slight frown on his normally cheerful face and found himself uncharacteristically counting the days until the end of the tour. After a mere four days he felt he had had enough of this particular group of troublesome tourists to last him a lifetime.

8

NIKOS was not the only one to be irritated by Brenda's constant staring and unwarranted and intrusive interest. Judith too was becoming increasingly conscious of the child's shifty glances in her direction — across the table at mealtimes, the hotel lobby where they all gathered before their outings and excursions, even from the farthest corners of the Archaeological Museum whence they all obediently trooped the following morning. With her recent encounter with Peter and Carol uppermost in her mind it was quite hard enough to concentrate on all the wonderful exhibits, the exquisite eggshell-ware from Kamares, the disk of Phaistos, the fascinating pottery figures and bowls, without the added strain of constantly meeting that unnerving stare from the other side of every glass case. Once or twice it seemed as if she hung back a little to try to stand beside her and looked on the verge of starting a conversation and Judith had even caught her mouthing some secret message to her across the bus yesterday. She'd tried to take no notice — she disapproved of such tactics — but had nevertheless interpreted the message as possibly, 'I'm on your side', which, she supposed ruefully, trying to suppress a sigh, was something of a comfort at least!

"That child is a menace to society," announced Betty to Judith as they both took refuge on a seat in the room where the marvellous finds from Knossos were displayed, waiting for the crowds crammed round the display-cases to disperse a little. Margs had elected to take herself round the museum with the help of her large, black book rather than join a guided tour and Betty, resplendent in a long, creamy-white cotton gown, simplicity itself in style, the neckline and sleeves smothered in multi-coloured, appliqué flowers, was finding the crush and the pace of the tour somewhat overwhelming. Though looking rather better today her blisters were still painful and Judith could tell that every unintentional jostle from impatient sightseers was causing her extreme discomfort.

"Bless you for making me buy this thing," Betty murmured, patting her hand and trying not to stare at the red marks that, in spite of the make-up, still showed faintly on Judith's cheek, "I honestly don't think I'd have been able to come out today if I'd had to wear my usual things — and later today it's Knossos! My whole reason for coming here! That really would have served me right, wouldn't it?"

Judith smiled at this — her first real smile of the day — in spite of the uncomfortable turmoil of her thoughts and Betty beamed at her in return.

"That's better," she said and, after glancing about to make sure they were not overheard she uttered confidentially, "and we're all on your side, my dear, over . . . you know, what happened yesterday." Judith raised her eyebrows and half-chuckled, thinking of Brenda's message mouthed across to her in the bus — and Betty continued, "We all saw it was an accident. You did very well not to punch that spoilt little madam in the teeth after the way she lashed out at you — I'm quite sure I should have done."

They fell silent as Peter and Carol, loosely hand-in-hand drifted into the room and stood staring into a glass-case full of tiny clay statuettes before being swallowed up by a huge crowd of German tourists, led by a guide with a voice like a trumpet and it was several minutes before they spoke again.

"He'll have his hands full with that one," declared Betty decisively as she struggled to get up from her seat, "Thank you, dear," and she shot Judith a knowing, sideways look. Judith did not respond but merely flushed a little and Betty's expression grew a trifle stern. They halted in front of the ivory model of a bullfighter leaping over the back of a bull and Betty's eyes gleamed as she thought ahead to their afternoon at Knossos itself. Judith did not reply and Betty's eyes narrowed as she noticed the bleak unhappiness in her young friend's face.

"I'm spoiling their holiday," Judith confided at last, biting at her lip in anxiety, fixing Betty with unhappy, tormented eyes, "let alone my own. Our both being here . . . it was all accidental whatever Carol seems to think. I hadn't the faintest notion they'd be on this trip and Peter couldn't possibly have known I would be. What I didn't realise . . . " her voice faltered a little, but as Betty maintained a sturdy silence and did not help her out she continued, " . . . what I didn't know was how I'd feel about seeing him again after all these years, I didn't know because I'd never thought about it." She glanced at Betty and could tell from her slow nods that

Rosemary had done her work well and that everybody who cared to, now knew about her former connection with Peter. She stared into a case of clay tablets inscribed with Minoan script without seeing a single one of them, "I gave him up once, Betty, years ago when I wanted my own life so I've no right to him now, no business to be thinking about him, acting like a fool . . ." For the second time in less than twenty-four hours she felt the approach of tears and dabbed furiously at her eyes, thankful they were now in a part of the museum where visitors tended to be few.

"And now you find you do love him after all," supplied Betty thoughtfully — and Judith frowned, considering, shaking her head and turning away.

"I don't know, Betty . . . I really don't know. He belongs to Carol now so there's no point in even . . ." She couldn't go on and Betty wisely did not pursue the conversation until they had glanced round the whole room and Judith had recovered herself a little.

"Well, I was never married myself," announced Betty as they began to make their way down the wide, stone staircase, "so I can't claim to be an expert on such matters." She stopped for breath and a party of unruly French schoolchildren went shrieking by, Judith fending them off to prevent further damage to Betty's delicate skin, "I can't tell if you're the right girl for him," she went on as they started off again and she looked thoughtfully at Judith through narrowed eyes, "but what I can tell is that Carol most certainly is not. She's beautiful — my God, I envy her that figure — she's got style, I grant you that, she'd be an asset to any man with his way to make in the world. But she'll tear your dreamy Peter to pieces, she'll lead him a dance and drive him crazy."

"Perhaps that is what he wants," replied Judith dolefully and Betty stopped suddenly in her tracks, causing a slight commotion as several people behind them collided with each other

— and she treated Judith to a severe, school-marmish glance.

"And is that what *you* want for him?" she challenged and Judith, embarrassed by the way people were casting curious glances towards them shrugged and shook her head, trying to hustle Betty down the remainder of the stairs and towards the great front-door.

"I've told you — it's not my business any more," she said as Betty obviously did not regard the subject as closed. "All I can do — what I must do — is keep out of their way and let them sort themselves out. That is all." Betty made no reply — but Judith felt as if her very silence were an answer, a silent criticism of her disappointing lack of action. What did Betty expect her to do? Throw down the gauntlet to Carol, challenge her to a duel, with Peter as the prize? Such a scenario conjured up a thrilling picture — but Judith could not even be certain in her mind whether she truly coveted the prize or not.

She followed the Wallis family onto the bus thoughtfully, forcing a tight smile at Brenda who poked her tongue out at Carol's back before complaining to her mother that she couldn't think of anything more boring than spending the entire afternoon among a whole load of ruins.

"You'll love it, darling," was Rosemary's reply and fortunately the noise of the engine starting up drowned Brenda's less-than-polite reply. Judith stared out of the dusty window as the bus rattled through the back streets of Heraklion and out onto the Knossos road, seeing nothing of the busy streets, the souvenir shops, the stream of buses, taxis and private cars all heading in the same direction, her mind full of the implications of Betty's words.

She — Judith — was the fly in the ointment. If she were not there, there would be no trouble between Peter and Carol and therefore no more unpleasantness for the rest of the party. But how could this be achieved? All her efforts to avoid them so far had ended in dismal failure. She sighed and stole a cautious look around the bus, a smile twitching at her lips as she noticed Betty and Margs poring over the big, black book, 'doing their homework'. George was asleep as usual and Jeremy had an uncharacteristically meditative air about him. He caught her eye and with his usual brazen conceit assumed her casual glance constituted an invitation and treated her to a sly wink . . . and all of a sudden Judith knew what she had to do!

The bus slowed at the end of the short drive to Knossos and Nikos issued tickets and instructions. A grim smile touched Judith's lips and a new determination stiffened her demeanour. Her solution to the problem might prove difficult to handle, might lead her into difficulties as yet unimaginable — but given luck and a little common sense there was no reason why her strategy should not work out beautifully. She sorted out her beach-bag, in which she had prudently packed her swimming-things (one never knew quite when Nikos would suddenly tell them of a suitable beach) beach-wrap, some plasters, sun-cream and a packet of currant biscuits and as they all descended from the bus and poured into a nearby *taverna* for a snack before tackling the 4,000-year-old labyrinthine maze of ruins she quickened her step to catch up Jeremy and managed to slip into a seat beside him — to his obvious delight.

She let him rattle on about this and that, agreeing with almost everything he said, even neglecting to remove her arm from where it rested on the table when she felt his warmly pressed against it. He began to look at her more frequently and she forced herself to look at him, trying to appreciate the too-white teeth and snapping china-blue eyes that narrowed from time to time as his gaze travelled critically over her body — and it was only when his bare leg began to entwine itself around one of hers that she jumped up, slipping her beach-bag carelessly over her arm, as if unable to stay away from the delights of the most famous of all Minoan sites for a moment longer.

He followed — as she had known he would, obedient as a puppy, all the while believing himself to be the one in charge. For three hours she led him round the palace, following a hilariously-translated booklet that had them both in quite genuine fits of laughter as they tried to follow the murdered English prose, often meeting other baffled little groups with the same booklet. Only Betty and Margs, armed with their big book knew exactly what they were looking at and whenever they spotted them they would wander over and get them to explain to them where they were. In this way they made haphazard progress but nevertheless saw all the main sights, the huge central courtyard where in ancient times the athletic bull-dancers had entertained King Minos and his royal relatives, the Throne Room, the Grand Staircase, the Giant Pithoi, even finding time to make their way down to the little theatre. From time to time huge white billowy clouds prettily covered the sky, sending Jeremy, who was a keen photographer, into frenzies of frustration as he tried to get his exposures just right and before long they began to build up into threatening grey banks growing up rapidly from an unhealthily bright-green horizon. By the time Betty and Margs and the little group that had gathered around them had also battled their way down to the theatre the grey had darkened further to a sinister black. The blue sky retreated swiftly before this menacing invasion and frowns were exchanged between members of the group as they rubbed their suddenly cold, bare arms, removed their sunglasses and asked each other what had happened to the weather.

As they listened to Betty giving her explanation as to the probable original use of the Sacred Way, Peter and Carol joined the group, the latter wearing an expression of mutinous displeasure. At their approach Judith deliberately thrust her arm into Jeremy's, leading him away from the two of them, only noticing out of the corner of her eye that Carol had left the group and sat herself down on one of the stone theatre benches, taking off her shoes and rubbing her feet with her hands. Brenda was behaving like a three-year-old, alternately jumping up and down the theatre seats or twirling round in the space where in days of yore the actors would have performed their tragedies, throwing her arms around and pretending to be a pop-star.

After a minute or two Jeremy also propelled Judith over to the theatre seats and they rested a moment, an anxious eye on the sky while Judith searched in her bag for the light cotton wrap that she knew was in there somewhere, glad she had thought to bring it with her. Brenda stopped her whirling and hovered nearby — hoping,

Judith supposed, that she was going to produce her packet of biscuits — and just as she'd extricated her wrap and flung it round her shoulders there was an excited cry from Nigel and the whole group rushed along the Sacred Way to see what he could possibly have found.

"Hoopoe!" he was repeating, pointing at a smart little black-and-white bird running about in short bursts of speed on the grass beneath the waving olive-trees and they all obediently peered at this phenomenon and tried to take photographs of it to show their envious friends back home. Brenda appeared just after it had flown away and as they all returned to the theatre that first warning, rustling breeze which inevitably brings large blobs of thundery-rain in its wake, began to whistle through the trees. In an instant the ground changed colour from dry orange to slippery black. Judith dashed to the stone seats to collect her bag and with one accord they abandoned Betty and Margs and the 4,000-year-old palace to the crows and sparrows and fled, their summer sandals slipping on wet paving-stones, their thin shirts and dresses clinging to their bodies.

It was actually quite comforting to Judith to have Jeremy's strong arms about her as they reached the bus and they flung themselves up the steps, laughing and gasping as they tried to shake the water from their clothes and hair, followed by most of the others in a similar state. Matthiou, from experience anticipating just such an event, had obligingly switched on the engine and got the heater going and soon they were only waiting for Betty, Margs, Peter and Carol to arrive. The former, draped in voluminous plastic capes without which neither of them would ever have dreamt of going anywhere, proved to be true heroines, buying everyone's souvenirs for them . . . and they were just about to re-enter the bus when the air of merriment cooled suddenly to a subdued sobriety. Dennis had spotted Peter, bedraggled, rain-sodden and exhausted, staggering along the pathway to the car-park — with Carol, her body wracked with sobs, in his arms!

"My God — she's hurt!" uttered Jeremy in a tone of extreme consternation and Judith noticed that beneath the rich suntan he had actually turned pale. He and Dennis hurtled out of the bus once more, almost fighting each other for the privilege of taking over Peter's burden for the last fifty yards or so — but Carol only buried her face in her lover's shirt and refused to be handed over. Rumour flew through the bus like the lightning that had just begun, to the accompaniment of rumbling thunder, to streak across the almost purple sky.

"Broken leg . . . twisted ankle . . . fainted . . . stung by a hornet!" Everyone except Brenda, who remained gravely mute put forward their explanation for Carol's distress — so when elucidation arrived, in the form of a furious enquiry from Peter, everyone was half-inclined to laugh.

"OK. Joke over," he began, gasping from his exertions, addressing the whole busload, while Carol tiptoed, damply, unhappily to her seat, "Who's pinched Carol's shoes? It must have been one of you." He raised his voice as titters and snatches of surprised conversation ran around the bus, "There was hardly anyone else there. Come on, hand them over — this is getting beyond a joke."

"You are having some bad luck this holiday, you poor thing," sympathised Rosemary, offering Carol a uselessly tiny hanky to try to wipe the mud off her feet — and everyone else chimed in, ashamed of themselves for laughing at her predicament, ashamed too of the slight disappointment they all felt when they realised she was not, after all, badly hurt.

"They're probably still down there somewhere," suggested Mark; then wished he hadn't as everyone looked at him as if he ought to offer to go back and look for them himself. But Peter remained adamant, standing at the front of the bus, his brow furiously knotted and his lips pressed into a thin, mean line.

"We — or rather I — searched every inch of the damned place," he informed Mark, unsmilingly, and tried to squeeze some of the muddy water out of the bottoms of his once-neat linen trousers, then casting another angry look around the bus, "For God's sake — shoes don't simply get up and walk off by themselves!"

"Goats eat shoes," Brenda piped up but was promptly shushed by her mother who, between claps of thunder, was heard to explain to her daughter that as there hadn't been any goats anywhere near the theatre they couldn't possibly have eaten Carol's.

"Didn't say they had," the odious child replied, "I was just making a general comment. Anyway, it was probably her." Judith saw, to her surprise that Brenda had indicated herself, once more to be wearily contradicted by her long-suffering mother. Judith quietly chuckled, then wished she hadn't as Peter had picked up Brenda's words and was looking across at herself and she didn't want him to think she was revelling in Carol's suffering. By this time the rain was pelting down and Nikos, as tactfully as possible, had to persuade Peter to move so that Matthiou could start for home. He wanted to get everyone back to the hotel before they began to feel the effects of the sudden drenching they had all had. Sunburn and blisters he could cope with — double pneumonia was a different matter. It was tough luck for that idiot girl to have lost her shoes — but he was in charge of the party and, knowing what weather like this could do to the roads, there wasn't a moment to lose. At last Peter was persuaded and he lumbered, crossly, down the bus to his seat where Carol was still trying to dry her feet. Matthiou turned the bus, peering through the smudged semicircle of comparatively clear glass made by the windscreen-wipers and headed cautiously back towards the city.

The trip normally took ten minutes. Today, water poured down the windows in a steady stream, the road became a river and the cavalcade of traffic which had all tried to leave Knossos at the same time, slowed to an anxious crawl. Everyone in the bus was tensely silent as the thunder crashed about them and lightning lit up the lines of buses, cars, lorries and wretched, unprotected motor-cyclists with vivid white light. Judith wiped her steamed-up window, thrilled to see the mountains stand out like stage-scenery against the dreadful sky. Gleams of sunshine, peeping through jagged breaks in the clouds miles away touched their peaks with gold and she held her breath in awe, forgetting all her problems, forgetting Peter, forgetting Carol and her shoes as the visions changed from moment to moment. She was chilly, she was damp, she was seated beside a man she did not particularly like, whose hot, unwelcome breath was on her neck, but her whole body nevertheless seemed charged with electric excitement and she felt her pulses race and the beat of her heart increase as the elements threw all their heaviest weapons upon the suffering earth.

Not everyone, it appeared, was similarly affected by the thrilling spectacle of the storm. Rosemary closed her eyes and moaned every time there was a clap of thunder. George, no doubt wondering what effect this downpour might have on their prospects for going down the Gorge, wore an expression as thunderous as the weather. And Carol, whilst dabbing at her ankle with Rosemary's handkerchief, gave a little scream as a spot or two of blood smeared over the once-white cotton.

"Anyone got a plaster?" Peter boomed around the bus, his expression one of extreme weariness — and his eye met that of Judith as she half-turned at the sound of his plea. Plasters. Yes, she had some, somewhere. The beach-bag was nearer Jeremy than herself, so she asked him to hand the whole thing over to Peter.

"They're in there, I know," she explained, "probably right at the bottom. Just rummage about, you'll find them."

Peter opened the bag, peering into its dark depths — and a curious silence settled on the bus as he remained, as if frozen, rather like a horse with its nosebag on, staring fixedly as if he had just encountered, not plasters, but the head of Medusa. Judith had turned back to look out of the window by this time, anxious not to miss a single second of the storm; so jumped with surprise when she received a sharp tap on the shoulder. She turned to look up into Peter's blazing, infuriated eyes! He said nothing — merely held the bag open for her to look inside. Confusedly she did so — and remained looking, as he had done, frowning with horrified incredulity, blinking in complete and utter amazement, her mouth half-open to protest.

There, on top of the biscuits, the plasters, the suncream and the now much-crumpled guide to Knossos, lay a pair of elegant, though dusty, ladies' sandals. They were not her own. Here, in her bag, by what means she could not even begin to imagine, were Carol's missing shoes.

9

FOR a moment the storm outside raged supreme as everyone inside the bus held their breaths; and Nikos closed his eyes in despair.

"Just keep driving," he murmured to Matthiou, who nodded grimly, narrowly missing a van which had skidded a few moments before and lay helplessly on its side across the road. Water was pouring down from the banks either side of the road, bringing sticks, stones, even sizeable rocks with it and at times the two torrents met in the middle, completely obscuring the surface. Still the lightning flashed, streaking in erratic forks across the leaden sky, followed by claps of thunder loud enough to waken all those long-dead Minoan spirits that haunted Knossos. But all this drama, all these efforts of nature to disrupt and disturb the normal course of life were lost on the occupants of that 'Island of Bliss' minibus. Their own particular storm, less noticeable to the outside world perhaps, but destined to have even more devastating repercussions for them than a mere combination of water, light and noise was about to break about their ears.

As Judith dared to raise her eyes from staring at the contents of her bag to meet Peter's challenging stare, she knew with utter certainty that he realised that she had not put them there. Words were not needed. A flash of honest comprehension seemed to leap across from her eyes to his and he said nothing as she drew the shoes out, handing them apologetically to Carol.

"I really haven't the faintest idea how they got there," she stammered, ineffectually trying to remove some of the orange dust of Knossos from where it was lodged along the seam. Carol, speechless with anger and shivering now from the effects of her soaking, shot out a hand and seized a handful of Judith's hair, twisting and tugging as hard as she could, fury lending her an almost maniacal strength. Taken by surprise, and in considerable pain, Judith yelled, falling across Peter as Carol pulled even harder and in an instant the bus was in an uproar. Half the passengers tried to pull Judith away — which only served to make matters worse — while the other tried to disengage Carol's hand from her hair. Somewhere in the middle was Peter, almost buried by struggling bodies and it was only his indignant bellow of rage as several elbows dug into his face and neck that restored some sort of order to the chaos. Nikos stood up, waving his arms about, trying to make himself heard above the din.

"Please, ladies and gentlemen — please, think of the driver, think of the danger . . . "

Nobody took the slightest notice of him. Carol, under pressure from Jeremy, Nigel and Rosemary had been forced to let go and sat, still speechless, almost stunned, staring at the strands of blonde hair clutched tightly in her hand. Judith, her hands to her head, just managing to fight down tears of pain and shock found herself almost smothered in patting, comforting hands, offered combs, hankies, sweets, wise words and helpful advice. Everyone who had lurched out of their seats to help in the emergency struggled back into them somehow and as Judith, covered with confusion and embarrassment and still trembling from the effects of shock, dared to look up from her seat to say thank-you for all the offers of help she noticed that Brenda, whom one would have expected to be gleefully in the forefront of any crisis was maintaining a very low profile indeed staring fixedly out of the window.

Brenda! She'd been running up and down the theatre-steps when they'd all made a dash to look at the hoopoe. She'd known those shoes were in her bag, Judith had heard her accuse her

to her mother. Of all the spiteful little
. . . At the next opportunity, once
she could get the little trouble-maker
on her own she'd have it out with
her, get her to own up, apologise to
both herself and Carol so that they
could get the situation sorted out.
A joke was a joke — but causing a
full-scale riot with danger to life and
limb was something altogether more
serious.

But Carol had not finished. She had
found her voice at last and, in spite
of the noise of the storm and the
rain on the roof it was obvious that
she and Peter were in the middle of
a tremendous verbal battle.

"For God's sake, Carol, of course
she didn't steal your shoes. If she had
do you think she'd calmly hand the bag
over for us to look in?"

"Yes, I do," countered Carol, her
voice rising dangerously, "that's exactly
what she would do. She wanted to
make me look a bloody fool." Everyone
tried to pretend they were not listening,

whilst straining their ears so as not to miss a word.

"No need for her to do that," came the swift reply. "You're managing to do that very successfully by yourself."

There was a short, icy silence, during which everyone held their breath and stared studiously out of the windows or looked unnecessarily in their bags. Even though she was sitting on the far side of the bus from her Judith automatically cringed, wondering what form Carol's retaliation would take this time, her head still smarting painfully from where the hair had been wrenched a few minutes ago. But Carol was controlled now, her eyes glittering, her voice level, dangerously soft.

"Right — now I know exactly what you think. Well, I'm sorry, Peter, but I've had just about as much as I can stand. I'm not staying on this bloody holiday a moment longer than necessary. As soon as we get back to Heraklion, Nikos, you can book us on the next plane home."

"You do just as you please," returned Peter, his voice low but ever so slightly trembling, "you've done nothing but grumble and complain ever since we got here. Really, Carol, what a fuss to make about a blasted pair of shoes. You go home if you want to — I can't stop you. Just don't expect me to come trotting after you, that's all."

Nobody heard Carol's reply, if indeed she made one. They had entered the city now and the scenes that met their eyes made even the most traumatic of personal events pale into insignificance besides the devastation the storm had caused. Everywhere was chaos. Water ran in continuous, muddy waterfalls down every hill and settled in vast, rubbish-filled lakes at every street-corner or crossroads. Cars, lorries and buses, abandoned by their drivers, their wheels lapped by the muddy water, their bodies constantly sprayed by mud thrown up by passing vehicles, littered and blocked the streets. The traffic-lights were either out-of-order or ignored, even the rule of the road had to go by the board when whole sections of it were obliterated by debris or abandoned cars. Somehow Matthiou kept going, never daring to stop completely and though it seemed an impossibility that anyone could actually arrive at a pre-arranged destination in such frightful conditions he managed to crawl right up to the hotel-door and with the combined efforts of Nikos, the hotel-manager, Mark and Nigel who all stood up to their ankles in swirling water, they managed to manhandle most of the bus-party into the building without too much damage to life and limb.

"Do the garden good," Judith heard Rosemary joke to Betty and Margs; and in spite of the trauma she had just experienced, she found herself wanting to smile. There was something very endearing about the British holiday-maker, determined to enjoy him or herself under the most adverse and trying circumstances. If only they were all like that, she pondered, managing to escape into the hotel well away from Carol — and cast her glance about, looking for a certain young lady with whom she intended to have some extremely strong words. But Brenda had had the good sense to make herself scarce.

★ ★ ★

For the rest of that day everyone avoided everyone else, going their separate ways once they had dried their clothes and recovered from the effects of the storm — and Nikos, sensitive to the tensions and potential splits in his group, issued individual meal-vouchers instead of organising the usual cheerful, get-together meal. The next day was supposedly free for people to choose their own amusement though it rarely worked out entirely free for Nikos, and this proved no exception. Two hours at least he spent on the telephone, which, after the heavy rain, would work only erratically, trying to book Carol onto a home-going flight — to no avail. Every plane was booked solid for the next few days though — as he tried to explain — she could always take up residence in the airport with her luggage and hope for a late cancellation.

"Like hell," had been her reply — and once she had been forced to accept the unpleasant situation, Nikos had then had to try to book another room for her as she refused utterly to remain with Peter, which was proving difficult as well as many hotels had already closed down for the winter. Eventually he had to give up his own room and move into lodgings across the road; then had to telephone the company to find out who should pay for what and how and when and so on and so forth. For this reason he had no time to spare for anyone else's problems and only just remembered in time to pin up the notice about a special 'Cretan Evening', with music and dancing to be held in the town-square later on that day and to which he strongly recommended everyone to go.

Judith caught the Wallis family reading this notice doubtfully as she left the hotel on her way to visit the Venetian Fort and craned her neck to look over their heads.

"Sounds like fun," she commented, "so long as the water dries up in time. Anyone going?"

Rosemary and Dennis exchanged glances and looked uncomfortable, while Brenda glowered at Judith, screwing up her mouth to bite her lip, making herself look even less attractive than usual.

"Well . . . we rather wanted to go out for a special meal tonight. Our anniversary, you know," ventured Rosemary, her eyes alighting on her unprepossessing daughter with affection, "only of course Brenda wants to go to this," she gave a high laugh and shot Judith a bright look, "so I expect we will." Brenda rewarded this piece of magnanimity by adopting a king-sized smirk on her pasty face which made Judith want to turn her over and smack her bottom. Heroically she resisted — and even more heroically, astonished at her own stupidity, she offered to take Brenda to the Cretan Evening herself to let Rosemary and Dennis celebrate properly on their own.

"My hair'll need washing," was all the gratitude Brenda showed — but Judith solved this problem too.

"Come to my room an hour or so before it's time to go out this evening and you can borrow my hair-dryer." She left the three of them staring after her, the parents with effusive gratitude, the daughter with suspicious caution — and took herself off for what she anticipated would be a glorious, solitary day.

She needed solitude — time to mull over what had happened yesterday, time to sort out her feelings and get to grips with the conflicting emotions that had robbed her of sleep again last night. She'd noticed Betty and Margs set off for the Fine Arts Museum, had heard Jeremy, Mark and Nigel making plans to play tennis, knew the Wallises and George were taking a taxi up to the Monastery at Vrontisiou, so reckoned she would remain undisturbed for most of the day at least. Feeling somewhat guilty at not equipping herself with a comprehensive history of the island now that she had a day in which to study it she slipped the copy of *Country Life* which she had brought with her as light reading but had not yet even opened along with her other bits and pieces into her bag and set off down towards the harbour, revelling in her freedom and the fact that for a few blessed hours she had absolutely no need to be tactful, understanding, patient or even mildly sympathetic to a single soul.

She walked along the stoutly-built, cobbled pier towards the yellow, circular fort, staring down at the rows of fishing-boats moored below it. The slap of water against wood and the light ringing sound of sheets against masts and the sharp, salty tang of the sea-breeze, all conspired to raise her spirits . . . and she dawdled in the sun, gazing at her own moving reflection in the rippling water. Damage caused by the storm was already being cleared away and tidied up by troops of street-cleaners armed with brooms and mops and once out on the fort and climbing up the ancient stone steps, Judith could see no evidence of storm-damage at all.

She wandered round, up into all the turrets, gazing out across the city and along the coastline, feeling herself deliciously cut off from the world, separated from civilisation by a hundred yards or so of clear, bright sea. London and the mad whirl of business, buses, fumes and crowds seemed blissfully far away, unreal. She found a sheltered nook in the corner of one of the towers and settled herself into it, facing the sun and closing her eyes. Bit by bit she felt herself relax into a dreamy state of semi-consciousness.

This glorious sun-washed island was the real world — for the moment anyway. Nothing else mattered — the only important things were the sun on her face, the peace and quiet, the gentle breeze and the calm, surrounding sea.

She was not really aware of how long she remained there, lazy in the sun — but eventually a shadow fell across her face and, automatically grabbing for her bag, she opened her eyes, trying to focus on the figure that stood before her, a surge of panic beginning to flood along her veins. The next moment she relaxed once more, shaking her head in relief, staring up at Peter with a mixture of pleasure and exasperation. Seeing him, however welcome his presence might actually be, reminded her too sharply of Carol.

"Carol managed to book her flight?" she asked, as Peter sat beside her, after lifting her feet off the stone seat to make room for himself. He shook his head, sighing and drawing his brows together in a frown.

175

"No flights — not for days. Nikos has done his best. Anyway she's gone off to play tennis with the three lads at that huge new holiday-complex we passed a few days ago on our way to Malia."

Judith did not reply. Peter got up, thrusting his hands into his pockets and looked over the parapet into the water below. The breeze blew his hair untidily all over his head and when he spoke his voice was low, unhappy — and he would not look Judith in the face.

"I suppose you don't want me bothering you either," he said at last . . . then half-turned with a cynical smile, "I don't seem to be flavour of the month just at the moment, do I?"

"It's not your fault, Peter — you know that," Judith replied, getting up and joining him at the wall, "I just don't want people to think . . . well, that I'm trying to steal you from Carol. If people see us together — especially now — they'll jump to conclusions, especially if they happen to be called Rosemary."

Peter allowed himself a cautious smile at this, then stared out to sea again, his gaze somewhere on the distant horizon.

"I suppose I've been a bit of a fool about Carol," he admitted, his expression thoughtful, puzzled. "You'd think by my age I'd know better." Judith did not speak but darted quick glances at him with half of her mind delighting that he was here with her with the other dreading the further complications his company might usher in.

"I suppose I thought she'd change," Peter continued, giving a bitter half-laugh. "I thought she might come round to my way of thinking and see that living in London with all the noise, the greedy people, the pressure to make more and yet more money all the time and do the other fellow down, well . . . I just thought I'd be able to persuade her that . . . oh, I don't know, simply that that kind of life is not enough."

"Give her time," murmured Judith as Peter fell into a studious silence, "she's young, she's still at the height of her career — you can't expect people to give up the kind of life that suits them just because *you've* had a change of heart. It's not fair."

Peter sighed and compressed his lips. "I realise that . . . I do," he said, "and if she's really keen to set up a modelling agency then that has to be done from London and I realise that too. But I can't wait for ever, Judith. I'm thirty-seven years old, old enough to be a grandfather! When you threw me over all those years ago I thought I'd never get over it, thought I'd remain a miserable bachelor for ever. I felt old then and that was ten years ago! Then Yvette came along and I thought all my troubles were over . . . and I suppose, if she'd lived they would have been." He paused a moment and Judith remained silent, " . . . but she died — and that was just my bad luck."

He paused again as a trickle of tourists began to clamber all over the fort and one or two of them came into the turret, waving their cameras, exclaiming at the view. With one accord he and Judith retraced their steps, wandering back across the pier, wrinkling their noses as the tempting smell of freshly-cooked fish reached their nostrils.

"Why don't we do something completely mad?" suggested Judith as they wandered down side-streets, almost too narrow for cars but perfect for motorscooters which zigzagged expertly down them disappearing into the brightness of the broad streets beyond — and Peter stopped, looking at her quizzically.

"Such as?" he enquired with a lift of the eyebrows and they both laughed.

"Why don't we hire one of those bike-things and get out into the countryside?" she suggested, her eyes lighting up with the thought of bowling along deserted little lanes with only rocks and sheep for company, "we could buy some bread and cheese and grapes . . ."

"Some retsina," suggested Peter, warming to the suggestion, "sounds brilliant — great idea. Have you any idea how to ride one of those things, by the way?"

In less than an hour they had settled on a visit to Achanes, bought their picnic, selected a bike that looked slightly less decrepit than most and each had had a trial ride up and down one of the side-streets. With much arm-waving and shouting of instructions, the hirers indicated a way of reaching the Knossos road, off which the road to Achanes lay, without encountering too much traffic and a minute or two later they were off with Peter taking first turn at the controls, Judith seated behind him clasping him firmly round the waist.

It was amazingly easy. Traffic was so chaotic anyway that any little errors went totally unnoticed and pedestrians seemed well-trained in the art of scooter-dodging. Even the much-used route to Knossos failed to dampen their enthusiasm and once they had branched off to Achanes the road became clear, almost traffic-free and the view as they climbed higher and higher into the mountains was quite breath-takingly beautiful. Time and again they stopped to look over the neat, golden fields and clumps of pine-trees or dawdled through shady villages, every garden ablaze with marigolds, petunias, geraniums, zinnias with huge exotic lilies, fresh and shiny after yesterday's rain, bordering every roadway.

Streams, usually a mere trickle by this time of year had been suddenly swelled and cascaded erratically down the hillsides, dampening the roads and laying the choking dust. A few miles short of Achanes they spied a tiny side-road and bumped along it, alone with the bees and kites circling high above them, not a soul in sight. Without a word Peter stopped the bike as they reached a small level plateau and they sat down in an orchard of peach-trees and gazed, struck dumb with amazement at the view before them. Down there, far below them, lay Heraklion — through a faint heat-haze they could make out the main streets, the harbour and the fort where they had sat that morning and beyond that the dark-blue line of the sea. Puffy white clouds, such as a small child might draw dotted the sky, innocently blue. Judith gazed and gazed hardly wanting to blink and miss a single marvellous moment and turned to Peter, her eyes as brilliant as the sky.

"This is what I shall always think of as Crete," she said, the words husky in her throat, "Vai was . . . Vai was wonderful, but this . . . Oh, Peter, we are so lucky to be up here . . . and not down there in the town."

Peter smiled, a huge, lazy embracing smile and sighed a deep, shuddering sigh. There was only the breeze, scented with thyme and the ever-present buzz of bees to witness his next move. His eyes half-closed, his breath coming in deep sighs, he placed both hands around Judith's eager face and drew her towards him slowly — but with determination. As their lips touched their arms went round each other urgently, wildly and they kissed and hugged as desperately as if this was their last moment on earth. Neither considered nor cared what this foolishness might mean. Kiss followed kiss until they were exhausted . . . and Judith had to turn her face away. Peter continued, kissing her neck, her arms, her shoulders, his warm mouth reaching ever closer to the soft skin around her breasts.

"We mustn't," she managed to gasp out as she felt his warm breath so enticingly on her skin and gradually managed to push his head away, "we really mustn't, Peter — you know we mustn't. It . . . it would be madness . . ." He drew his head back a little at this, focusing on her anxious face with quizzical eyes and broke into a slow, engaging grin.

"You were the one who wanted to do something completely mad, remember?" he reminded her, teasing her with a lock of her own hair, trying to brush it across her lips, tickling her ears. Then, realising that she meant what she said, with a grunt he managed to roll himself away from her and tried to distract himself by rummaging through her bag.

"Hm . . . no shoes today," he complained, ironic disappointment in his tone of voice and Judith collapsed in helpless giggles as he seized the bunch of grapes and began pelting her with them one by one. Eventually he calmed down and they ate their picnic with decorum, washing it down with retsina and mineral water and finishing off the rest of the grapes. When they had finished Peter fumbled in the bag again and produced Judith's by now rather stained and mangled copy of *Country Life*.

"I shall read this while you take your siesta," he announced and Judith acquiesced gratefully — in any case she could hardly keep her eyes open a moment longer. She lay in the shade with her eyes shut, listening to the minute sounds of insects among the grass, the distant sound of traffic on the main road far away, the comforting sound of pages being turned and the occasional grunt or envious whistle from Peter as his eyes alighted upon some dream house beyond his means. Gradually all sounds ceased — and Judith fell peacefully asleep.

10

"JUDITH . . . I've found a house!"

Judith emerged regretfully from a sweetly refreshing sleep to feel Peter shaking her by the shoulder. She struggled up, ready to complain at the unwelcome disturbance, her hair dotted with the dried flower-heads of tiny grasses and opened her eyes to see Peter standing, staring as if transfixed at a page of photographs in her magazine. His hands were trembling with excitement so that the pages shook and as she glanced over his shoulder, still mazed by sleep, she could see nothing but a muddle of pictures and print.

"Oh, good," she replied grudgingly and prepared to roll over into a more comfortable position and continue her siesta. But Peter rolled her back again, unceremoniously heaving her up into a sitting-position, thrusting the magazine right under her nose. The sun shone, glinting off the bright, glossy pages and Judith blinked like an owl disturbed by daylight.

"This one — that's exactly what I'm looking for," she heard him say, with a catch to his voice that alerted her to the fact that he was deadly serious and not just playing the 'dream-houses' game. She pulled herself together, shaking the sleep from her eyes and tried to concentrate on the picture almost obliterated by his stabbing finger, reading aloud slowly as the print danced and jumped before her.

"Converted, stone-built coach-house and stable-block . . . original eighteenth-century clock-tower . . . splendid galleried living-room . . . five bedrooms (who on earth do you propose to put in all those bedrooms?) . . . small gatehouse. Peter, it sounds fantastic! But why the sudden interest in horses?"

"Fathead," he replied, affectionately, seizing the magazine from her, frowning earnestly as he scanned the page again, "they're not stables any more, that's all part of the house . . . that's where the five bedrooms come into it. Listen a moment . . . modern fitted kitchen, that's a relief anyway, one acre of interesting garden — that probably means an untameable wilderness." He laid the magazine down on his knees, gazing abstractedly into the distance, his lips pursed in deep thought. Judith brushed a small, shiny beetle off his collar just as it hesitated on the brink between the pale-green cotton material and the rich golden-brown of his skin and, hardly realising what she was doing, she pressed the back of her hand softly against his neck. It was soft, tender and warm — just like the expression in his eyes as he turned to look at her, bending his head down suddenly to trap her hand beneath his chin.

They looked at each other in silence for a few seconds, an uncertain wariness in their expressions. Then Peter, with a half-laugh, released her hand and she let it fall back into her lap and, unconsciously, heaved a huge, satisfying sigh. Her eye fell on the page of houses again and she took in the name of the estate agents with a sudden flickering of interest. It was the one Stella, her best friend since boarding-school days, worked in, dealing mostly with oil-rich Arabs looking for properties in Mayfair and Belgravia.

"If you're really keen on that place I could try giving Stella a buzz," murmured Judith, "she'd pass the message on to — where is it? Shropshire? Devon? They'll have a branch-office in Tavistock, somewhere like that, I shouldn't wonder."

Peter had stood up by this time, stretching his arms above his head, letting the warm wind blow through the thin cotton of his shirt and he took a pace or two around their picnic-place, obviously deep in thought.

"You see, it looks the sort of place where . . . well, where I could

189

get on reasonably undisturbed with my furniture-restoration. London's too . . . too distracting, I'm too busy buying and selling and finding new customers to be able to spend time putting beautiful pieces of work to rights. It breaks my heart sometimes to have to sell on a heavenly Chippendale bookcase or a bureau or long-case clock that really requires expert attention."

Judith drew her knees up to her chin, folding her arms around them and looked up at him with a thoughtful frown.

"You could use the 'splendid galleried living-room', if it really is splendid, as a sort of saleroom. Antiques would look right in a place like that. Then people could come and see how they might really look in their own homes. Much better than a shop or saleroom in London."

Peter stopped pacing and looked directly at her, his eyes shadowed in thought.

"Brilliant", he uttered, hitting one

fist into the palm of his other hand. "A sort of living shop. I'm sure it would work — so long as we got enough customers. They might never find us in the back of beyond."

Judith looked away, suddenly uneasy at the way he was so freely using the plural. Wasn't he assuming just a little too much? He knew that Carol was determined not to leave London, so why . . . ? The same thought must have just struck Peter as he strode over to her, crouching down beside her, placing his hands urgently on her knees, his eyes narrow but alight with hope.

"I mean you and me, Julu — together we could make a go of it, you with your flair for interior design and me with my idiotic urge to mend things. God knows what state this place is really in — perhaps your friend Stella would be honest with you — but even if it needed doing up, well in a way that would be an advantage, I mean . . ."

"Peter, stop it!"

At the look of determination in Judith's eyes Peter trailed into silence and turned away, walking a few paces away from her — then turned, surveying her with serious eyes and trembling lips.

"Sorry . . . sorry . . . stupid of me. We . . . we've been through all this sort of thing before, haven't we? It's just that — oh, I don't know Judith, but it just seems so right. I can see us there, there in that house; you'd have your own life, of course you would, an advisory service, something like that. I know it would have to be on a smaller scale than in London, but . . . "

"Peter — I said stop it! It's not fair." Judith stood up and walked away from him, holding her face in her hands. It was so tempting just to rush at him and say yes, yes, we could do that — but it was not twenty-four hours since he was deeply committed to Carol and in another twenty-four they might be reconciled and this whole idyllic dream be brushed aside as a mere irrelevant fancy. Yes, she did see that it could work — it *could* work. But she was not going to let the sensuous, seductive scents of the Cretan countryside tempt her into a dreamworld which might suddenly evaporate into the air like the morning's dew. She had had too much experience of the world to agree to rush headlong into a new life without considered, careful thought. She heard Peter's steps behind her among the brittle grass and herbs and drew in great gulps of aromatic air, bracing herself for what she knew would be another seductive onslaught upon her better judgement. He stood behind her, his arms around her, trapping her own arms, resting his chin upon her silky head, pressing kisses into her hair in the pauses between his words.

"We are right for each other, Judith . . . we always were, surely you remember. I just wish . . . oh, I don't know what I wish . . . I just wish you weren't so . . . so insufferably sensible."

And I wish you weren't so insufferably persuasive, she wanted to scream, longing to turn round, fling all her protective reasonableness away and cast herself into his care. But she held back, merely relaxing a little against his strong body and smiled a half-regretful smile.

"Thank you for asking, Peter . . . and I haven't said no. It's just that I can't possibly say yes. Not with Carol still . . . well, still . . ."

"OK — enough said . . . and I do understand." Peter sighed briefly, then releasing Judith set about briskly tidying up their picnic-things, packing the remains back into their bags, his face thoughtful, his eyes still far-away. With some reluctance he folded up the magazine, slipping it into Judith's bag and briefly shook his head.

"Probably sold by now anyway," he murmured, his voice gruff with regret; and he frowned slightly at his own tone of voice, shaking his shoulders and forcing a smile to show Judith that he really didn't care one way or another if it was — but she was not fooled. They sauntered back to the track where the motor-scooter awaited them and Judith took the controls this time, deliciously conscious of Peter's encircling warmth as he tucked his tall body in behind hers as they started off down the stony track. They forged on to Achanes, admiring the waterfalls along the way and sat for more than an hour at an outdoor café beneath a canopy of brilliant bougainvillaea drinking iced coffee, laughing, talking and watching the world pass infinitely slowly by. The conversation inevitably turned to discussion of the other members of their party and many sets of ears should have been set burning that afternoon.

"They're probably talking about us as well," uttered Peter in an effort to justify their giggles and less than complimentary remarks and Judith fell momentarily serious again as she wondered if anyone would think to link their two absences and what effect this might have on Carol. She really didn't want to be the cause of any more unpleasant scenes — it made things so difficult for the other holiday-makers.

"I wonder what George is making of the monks' hospitality at Vrontisiou," she murmured uttering a silent prayer of thanks to the Wallises for persuading him to go with them — there was something pathetic about that fat, ill-mannered man that made her feel she wanted someone to take pity on him — just so long as it did not have to be herself.

"With any luck he might decide to stay up there for ever," suggested Peter hopefully and once more they descended into giggles, frightening a thin, yellow dog that had taken up refuge in the shade of their table.

"What . . . and miss the Gorge!" spluttered Judith, throwing the dog the end of a piece of pastry she had left on her plate and she turned to Peter with a puzzled expression on her face.

"Have *you* any idea why he has this fixation about going down the Gorge?

It seems so unreasonable in a person of his dimensions."

Peter called the waiter over, ordering two more coffees and gazed across at Judith thoughtfully.

"Now . . . that's interesting. Remember when you ladies were disporting your nakedness to all the world at Vai . . . ?"

" . . . not only ladies," interjected Judith but Peter ignored this and carried on, "well, we had to do something to restrain George from staring pop-eyed at all that flesh — we thought he'd get us all arrested — so we got him talking about why he'd come to Crete and quite honestly, Julu, it was all rather touching. Apparently his father had been parachuted into Crete in 1941 and had fought alongside the Australians and New Zealanders at Malame — I think there's an optional trip there later in the tour — and had been among the thousands that tried to use the Samaria Gorge as an escape-route." Judith began to nod and Peter went on, "Actually hundreds, if not thousands, managed to get to Chora Sfakion and were rescued but apparently poor old George's father rather ignominiously fell headlong down a cliff, broke his back and his companions, in their mad rush to escape the Germans couldn't possibly take him with them. All they could do was carry him into a little chapel — there are several of them down there — and leave him to die. That was the last news that was ever heard of him, God knows what happened to the poor bloke." Peter fell silent for a moment and looked away from Judith as he took a sip of his drink.

"So George must only have been six or seven," she murmured, shaking her head in wonder, "and now he wants to see where his father died. But why has he waited so long? Why not come when he was fit and healthy?"

Peter wrinkled his brow and shrugged.

"From what we could gather he was married to a rather dominating wife who refused to set foot out of England and wouldn't let him either. She died last year so this holiday is really the first taste of real freedom he's ever had."

"A pilgrimage," murmured Judith, her eyes, to her embarrassment, beginning to mist over at the thought of that one steadfast idea remaining locked in that unprepossessing, stout little man's soul for nearly fifty years; and she looked suddenly directly at Peter. "Peter, I do hope that chapel is still there — it would be too awful if . . . " but Peter was already nodding reassuringly.

"It's OK — we checked with Nikos. It is still there, the peace and quiet of it ruined by visitors of course, as is the whole length of the Gorge. I honestly don't think George quite realises that the lonely, terrifying crack in the cliffs that had provided a refuge for so many soldiers has become such a tourist attraction. But that's not really the point. We know the chapel's there . . . question is, will George make it that far?"

Judith frowned, pressing her lips together with determination.

"He'll make it, Peter. Even if we all have to take turns to carry him. We'll get him there somehow. We've got to." Idiotically she found herself weeping, to the amazement and concern of a stout Cretan couple at the next table who had been eyeing them with the kindly sympathy that happy old couples reserve for happy young ones.

Peter stretched out a hand, patting her arm, passing her a crumpled handkerchief with which she dabbed furiously at her eyes.

"You're amazing — d'you know that?" he murmured, "to shed tears for a none-too-fragrant elderly man of whose existence you were totally unaware until a few days ago." He narrowed his eyes regarding her keenly. "And I noticed how you took charge of Betty and her sunburn and you always seem to be in the right place when Margs needs a bunk-up into the bus." He took her hands in his and smiled slowly, one of those huge, enveloping smiles — and the elderly couple wagged their heads knowingly, treating Peter and Judith to a series of tremendous, stagey winks. They might have remained, hands clasped, for ever if Judith had not caught a glimpse of her watch and with a shock realised that it was fast approaching five o'clock.

"Oh, Lord, I've promised to take that frightful child to the festival tonight — and she's supposed to be washing her hair in my room first." She got up, brushing the light dusting of pollen which had fallen from the flowers above them off her arms. Peter rose too, following her to the scooter.

"I thought you couldn't stand the brat," he commented as they mounted their steed once more. Judith chuckled, leaning close to Peter as he started up the bike and they began to move off.

"An ulterior motive, I'm afraid," she confided as they began the steady downhill, twisting journey back to Heraklion. "I suspect her strongly of having put Carol's shoes in my bag yesterday and I just want to find out why she's such a beastly little trouble-maker. I could've been scalped because of her — very nearly was!"

Peter made no reply — she was not even sure that he had heard her and they spoke no more. The journey down towards the coast, though even more hazardous than forging their way up, was even more spectacular as the sun sank in the sky, disappearing behind bluffs of rock, then blazing out again, the heat hitting their skin with an almost tangible force. As they passed the track which led to their picnic-place, Peter slowed and both turned their heads simultaneously, remembering those stolen moments — and Judith, suddenly regretful though not quite understanding why, printed an apologetic kiss on Peter's back and rubbed her hand briefly against his warm, bumpy spine. They did not speak but each guessed at the other's thoughts — and it was a strangely silent couple that returned the bike to the hire-shop, paid for the petrol and strolled back through streets just coming alive again after the heat of the afternoon.

Neither mentioned the coach-house — but Judith resolved to put a call through to Stella just as soon as there was the opportunity. Although the magazine was a week or two old by now there was always a chance that a house of that type which was certainly not everybody's cup of tea, would still be on the market and if it would please Peter . . . well, why shouldn't she try to help an old friend?

She only just had time to have a quick shower and change into a low-necked, pale green cotton dress before Brenda came knocking at her door. Judith sighed and braced herself before letting her in — secretly she had been hoping she might have forgotten or made other plans. But, bold as brass, she walked in and began commenting on all Judith's possessions.

"Hey, young lady, I thought you wanted to wash your hair," Judith reminded her as Brenda flung herself across the bed, narrowly missing creasing the white stole she had put out to wear with the green dress, flicking over the pages of *Country Life* with an expression of disgust on her peaky face. "You won't find any photos of pop-groups in there, I'm afraid. Come on, I'll wash it for you — will your mum mind if you wear it loose, it'll look lovely, especially if we pop on a bit of make-up as well?"

Brenda eyed Judith cautiously at this, sniffing a little uncertainly and Judith laughed, but not unkindly, at her dubious expression.

"I promise I won't make you into a scarlet woman," she reassured her. "We'll put on just enough to make sure Nikos asks you for a dance." Brenda blushed scarlet indeed at this and Judith had a moment of panic as she realised how accurately her casual remark had struck home — and she didn't even know if Nikos would be there! "or someone just as handsome and charming," she added hastily.

"I don't think Mum . . . " began Brenda; but Judith bore her off to the bathroom and for the next half-hour or so it was like being back at school, swopping girl-talk, exchanging ideas on hair-styles and clothes while the soapy water flew all over the bathroom and somehow the topic of Carol's shoes lost its importance. Once Brenda's hair had been towelled dry then finished off with Judith's hair-dryer it lost its dull brownness and gleamed almost gold. With gentle coaxing, small wisps in front arranged themselves attractively around the girl's thin, eager face and Judith took her by the shoulders, making her stare at herself in the mirror. Instinctively she began to push the hair as usual straight back off her face.

"Leave it," ordered Judith, quite sharply, and Brenda obeyed, eyeing her reflection with cautious doubt. Judith searched amongst her possessions and produced a few fine hair-grips, pushing the hair gently forward to create a soft outline, fastening it firmly and allowing the rest to flow appealingly over Brenda's bony shoulders.

"Just a touch more with the dryer and you'll be fine." She switched it on and was busily working on a few damp patches when she heard someone at her door, which Brenda, in her casual teenage way had left wide open.

"Think I could borrow that dryer, Rosemary?" She heard a voice call and, somewhat puzzled, both Judith and Brenda emerged from the bathroom to see Carol, flushed and triumphant from her day's tennis, standing just inside the room. She started and flushed when she saw Judith and began to leave the room.

"Sorry — Jeremy saw Brenda come in here and so we thought it was Rosemary's room — sorry to bother you." Judith left Brenda, stepping quickly across to Carol, looking her squarely in the eye.

"Don't be daft," she said, using much the same tone to Carol as she had to young Brenda. "Of course you can borrow my dryer." You look as if you need it, was what she'd like to have added as Carol's dark hair was damp with perspiration. "If you could just hang on a minute while I finish off this young lady. There's a magazine on the bed. We won't be more than a second or two."

It was obvious from Carol's expression that her desire for a dryer was proving greater than her pride and after a moment's hesitation she entered the room, sat down on the bed and began flipping over the pages of *Country Life*.

"Just like a real salon," remarked Brenda, giggling — and the sudden cheerful expression, lighting up her eyes, transformed her normally discontented face and she looked cheekily up at Judith, "I hope you won't expect a tip."

"I certainly shall — a huge one,"

joked Judith and switched off the dryer, wrapping the cord around it and handing it over to Carol. She took it doubtfully and shot a swift look at Judith, then another at Brenda who could not take a hint if it was handed to her on a plate so stayed, plumping herself down at Judith's dressing-table, putting her face first on one side then the other, the better to admire her new, attractive looks. Carol frowned and cleared her throat, scowling nervously.

"Look — I'm sorry about yesterday. I behaved extremely badly. I . . . well, I was in a bit of a state anyway and then . . . well, thinking you'd stolen my shoes was just about the last straw." Brenda stopped admiring herself and sat very still as Judith accepted Carol's apology with praiseworthy warmth.

"It's OK," she heard her say, "don't give it another thought. I expect it was the thunder — funny how thunder can make people do the most peculiar things . . . eh, Brenda?"

Brenda turned huffily, snapping a

sly look at Judith, then blushed scarlet and — after a hideous moment of silence — she began to cry. Carol looked into Judith's eyes with sudden comprehension; then at Brenda with a furious frown. Judith shook her head briefly at her, then turned to the child with brisk annoyance.

"Oy, don't do that. We're going to make your face up now and we can't do that if your eyes are all gungey and your cheeks soaking wet. What do you suggest, Carol, with her colouring? Beige foundation with a little rose blusher? What about eye-shadow? What colour dress will you be wearing?"

For a few minutes the three of them were united in a common interest. Brenda forgot to cry and Carol forgot to leave as together they worked a transformation on the girl. Carol, as a model, was an expert on make-up and by the subtlest of means she brought out highlights of the face that Judith — and especially Brenda — had never suspected were there.

After they had finished Judith raided her mini-bar for fizzy lemonade and they sat, a companionable trio, on the bed, sipping, laughing and generally enjoying themselves. Brenda got hold of *Country Life* again and flipped through its pages, reading out prices with sarcastic amazement from time to time.

"Where would you live, Judith, if you had a million pounds?" she asked, not waiting for an answer, "I'd buy one of those villas in Majorca, make all my friends jealous. Where would you live, Carol, if you had a million pounds?"

Carol smiled ironically — which made Judith suspect that she might indeed be possessed of such a sum or at least have access to it — and she took the magazine from Brenda, scanning the pages with a critical eye.

"There's a nice-looking penthouse just off Park Lane," she remarked tentatively, "oh, and quite a decent townhouse near Sloane Square — yes, I wouldn't mind either of those, I suppose." An imp of mischief darted into Judith's brain and instead of suppressing it firmly and chasing it away as she knew she should, she gave into temptation, despising herself heartily for doing so.

"What about this one," she suggested as if her eyes had just alighted on it, "a converted, stone-built coach-house and stables . . . gatehouse . . . acre of interesting gardens. How about that for your country retreat?" Carol threw back her head and screamed with laughter.

"You must be joking!" she said, an expression of horror passing over her fine features. "Just think of all those spiders! And a garden! I haven't pulled a weed up since I was about three — and even then I think it was a delphinium. I remember my grandmother being most frightfully cross about it."

They all had a good laugh. Then Carol left, clutching Judith's hair-dryer and Brenda left a minute or two later to get changed. Judith stayed staring at the photograph of the coach-house, her mind a muddle of emotions, yet with a slight smile touching her lips. She sat there, quietly thoughtful, for many minutes. Then, on an impulse, after glancing at her watch and doing frantic mental-arithmetic to try to work out what time it was in England she decided that there was a good chance that someone as dedicated to making money as Stella would still be at work. Feeling strangely wicked and after the merest moment of hesitation she picked up the telephone and asked for an outside line.

11

THE Cretan festival was a wild success with much dancing, drinking, singing of noisy songs, ringing of bells, kissing and cuddling and rhythmic stamping of feet. Amazingly, with her hair flowing free and the touches of make-up, the excitement of the music, clapping and stamping, the lights strung across the street, the balloons, paper-flowers and fireworks, a new Brenda, bright, lively and talkative emerged like a butterfly, trying out her wings for the very first time. She was so animated by the evening's proceedings that when Judith suggested that it was time they made their way back to the hotel she begged to be allowed to stay away from her parents' dreary company a little while longer.

"Please — just a little walk down to the harbour," she pleaded, tossing back the hair and, with a quick glance at her watch, then up at the starry sky, Judith relented. It was a beautiful night — and couldn't do any harm.

"Come on then — just for ten minutes." They set off, wandering down the narrow streets towards the thick, encircling city walls, lit for this special occasion by fairy-lights and ventured onto the pier where the cool breeze blew. There were a few seats facing the harbour — each one occupied by loving couples who had managed to evade their chaperons and, slightly uncomfortable at passing these ecstatic demonstrations of passion Judith persuaded Brenda to walk a little more quickly as far as the fort. Then they turned to retrace their steps. It was when they were on their way back and had passed most of the entwined couples for a second time that Brenda, with all the tact of a ten-ton truck stopped and pointed at one seat in particular.

"Oh, look!" she said, her voice

carrying clearly on this calm, star-studded night and Judith frowned anxiously, rather wishing she had not agreed to this nocturnal adventure. What *had* the wretched girl seen now? Whatever it was it was sure to be something of which Rosemary and Dennis would heartily disapprove. But Brenda had faltered a little as two faces, pale in the evening light, turned briefly towards them and even by starlight Judith could make out the flash of a perfect set of snow-white teeth and she hustled Brenda along past Jeremy and the girl he was entangled with, pretending that she at least had not seen him. It was none of their business what a healthy young male tennis-star got up to on his holiday, especially when his hopes of her own co-operation in that direction had received nothing but rebuff.

"Didn't you see who he was with?" whispered Brenda, urgently, once they were safely past — and she kept twisting her head round, trying to keep the couple in sight.

"No, I did not," replied Judith, steering her across the road, hoping they would reach the hotel before Brenda's parents decided to send out a search-party to rescue their innocent, unsullied child. She sensed Brenda's sudden eagerness and sense of importance as she almost burst with her news. She tugged at Judith's arm to get her to stop for a moment and they halted briefly.

"Come on then — amaze me," she said jokingly. But at Brenda's reply it was Judith who then stood stock-still for a moment, her mouth half-open with surprise, a rush of incredulous new possibilities invading her mind.

"I jolly well will amaze you," Brenda had assured her, her eyes alight with the thrill of being the first to discover a juicy new scandal with which to liven up the rest of the holiday — and she'd paused just long enough to give her words their full, dramatic effect, " . . . because it was Carol!"

★ ★ ★

The road through Mines down to Gortys and Phaistos was wet and muddy but not impassable and Nikos's anxieties about the remainder of the trip subsided as the sky remained a clear, unblemished blue. They had picnic-lunches today so a few fine hours were essential if the party were to remain in good spirits. With the last tour of the season there was always this danger of storms breaking, yet he had known years when the weather stayed fine for two or three weeks into November and, had he known, he could have made himself a bit more money. It was a chancy business, tourism. Politics, natural disasters, airport strikes, a hotel-fire, all could put people off and prompt them to cancel their holidays, causing disruption and hardship to a whole chain of service-industries right down to the grape-seller who trudged up and down the beach all day long and the little boys who cleaned cars for the car hire shops.

Their schedule that day was so tight that there was little time or opportunity for the group to give him much trouble. He led them round the Roman remains at Gortys and the Minoan palace at Phaistos at a rate that ruled any activity apart from breathlessly chasing after him out of the question. The pace of the day's sight-seeing seemed to exhaust everyone and their energy did not revive until the following day when they arrived at the pretty, quiet town of Rethymnon.

By now, even without Brenda's broad hints it was appearing obvious to everyone that Carol and Jeremy were fast becoming an inseparable pair. There was no more talk of going back to England which relieved Nikos's mind considerably . . . But this new alignment brought problems for Judith as Peter now assumed that this gave him *carte blanche* to monopolise herself. She was less certain and indeed occasionally hostile to the idea that they should now automatically drift together.

"I can't decide whether I need him or not," she confided to Rosemary as they strolled in a loosely-knit group around the narrow alleyways of the town, gazing upwards at the plant-bedecked wooden balconies that seemed at times almost to meet above their heads. A half-open door would occasionally reveal a glimpse of the greenest of green courtyards, with tiled floor, splashing fountains and verandah of vine-covered trellis, hidden oases of cool, secret worlds behind high, peeling shabby walls that looked as if they had not been painted for the past fifty years. Rosemary crooned sympathetically, uttering well-worn platitudes about marriages being made in Heaven and everything turning out for the best.

"I hope my Brenda will meet a nice young man one day," she continued, doubtfully, as Brenda took long strides to catch up with Nikos and Judith smiled, "but not too soon." Judith smiled again, regretfully this time. That was the trouble. What did one do if one met one's true love (if such a creature existed) too early in one's life?

"Life is a problem," Rosemary observed, unhelpfully, and Judith walked on ahead a little staring up at the huge dome of the mosque within the Venetian fortress, dotted with a row of pigeons outlined against the sky like a row of dumpy statues. Beneath her feet the pine-needles were dry and slippery and she gulped in the hot resiny smell that wafted across the site, the breeze drying her skin, bleaching her hair to palest silver. She crept into the shade below a vast pine-tree, sitting with her back against the trunk watching the rest of the group pass to and fro before her eyes like dolls in a puppet-show — and as Peter passed, chatting affably to George, red-faced and already exhausted, her heart bumped erratically and she scolded herself for giving in to idiotic female frailty.

She sat perfectly still, confident that she was invisible in the shadows — but by some kind of second-sight Peter spotted her and, with a word to George, left him to struggle up the steep pathway on his own and walked over to the pine-trees, growing larger, ever larger in Judith's vision until he dominated the entire space, cutting out the sunlight, towering over her like a giant. She moved up, leaving him room to settle down beside her and together they looked out across the sunlit spaces dotted with moving figures, like two animals peeping out from the safety of their den. After a few minutes of companionable silence, Peter turned to look at Judith.

"You never told me what you managed to find out about that coach-house," he reminded her, half-accusingly, picking pine-needles gently out of her hair, " . . . or did you forget to phone?"

"I didn't forget — and Stella phoned me back last night." She looked Peter full in the face before replying, noticing the eager but well-controlled interest that shone out of his eyes.

"Well?" he encouraged, a slight frown between his eyes telling Judith that he was mentally preparing himself for disappointment.

"Well it's not sold — yet," she admitted and looked away, turning her attention to a couple of mouse-brown sparrows that had landed, squabbling, in the branches just above them, "but . . . !"

She paused a moment, giving herself time to choose her words with care, while Peter strove to restrain his impatience.

"Go on . . . but what?" he repeated and Judith, her mind made up turned and looked directly into his eyes.

"But," she repeated, "there is someone else very keen on the place who has already made an offer. That's really all I know."

"Damn . . . and blast! I hate whoever it is already!" replied Peter, his expression changing from anxious anticipation to irritation and disappointment and he tried to stand up, banging his head on a branch, bringing down another shower of dead pine-needles upon Judith's head. "Isn't that just my luck?" They crept out from under the tree and Peter walked off with such long strides that Judith had almost to run to catch up with him, reaching him as he paused beside the stout, outer wall. They stood with their backs against the warm stone as forty or so Japanese tourists passed them by, their feet kicking up little spurts of dust as they went — and she glanced anxiously up into his face. Disappointment, frustration, even annoyance were there and she heaved a sigh, wondering if she had been wise to tell him the news. Together they gazed down at the sea and the long, long beach below, already liberally dotted with groups of bathers and picnickers preparing for another day of soaking up the sun. Stella, for old times' sake, had managed to find out the true condition and location of the house for her and it had all sounded very satisfactory — in fact it had sounded well-nigh perfect.

"It's only an offer," she reminded him as they gazed down over the delightful jumble of red roofs below, "All sorts of things can happen to offers. Don't let it spoil your holiday." Peter dropped a light kiss on the top of Judith's warm, silky head.

"Well, there's not a lot I can do from here — so, as you say, better to forget it and get on with enjoying all this." They looked down at the crazy pattern of little streets below them, the occasional large building standing out oddly, areas of parkland showing up as dark, shadowy patches — and both heaved deep, contented sighs. Far below them, tiny from their viewpoint, they spotted Betty and Margs ambling slowly along one of the streets towards an outdoor café. They had got up early that morning and 'done' the sights before the rest of them had even finished breakfast.

"They're amazing," murmured Judith, shaking her head in wonder as they watched them settle down at a table and the inevitable black book was produced, "in spite of their age and infirmities I think they're enjoying this trip more than all of us put together." Peter nuzzled his chin into Judith's hair and made a playful bite at her ear, then turned her towards him looking at her with a scowl of mock severity.

"Now that's an assertion I would like to dispute," he uttered and, his eyes half-closing as he gazed at Judith's lively face, her expression bright with fun, he gave a little, helpless grunt and, oblivious of the proximity of several German holiday-makers armed with an amazing array of photographic equipment he enfolded her in yet another long, slow, almost suffocating kiss.

★ ★ ★

During the next two days they visited two monasteries, lazed on Rethymnon's vast sandy beach and tackled a five-mile hike across the crisp, dry hillside to a village where the whole population turned out to welcome them with song and dance and an alfresco meal of spit-roasted lamb, smothered in herbs and served with flaps of home-made bread. This last expedition allowed Nikos to assess the potential of his clients. He was already dreading the task of having to explain to Betty and Margs that he felt the Gorge trip would be too much for them when they — and Carol — relieved him of his responsibility by voluntarily deciding not to go. "We'd much prefer to see the scenery from the bus as it goes over the mountains to collect you all," Betty assured him to his immense relief and really, with those three taken care of George was his only problem. Everyone else had the potential to manage perfectly easily. But George — and the prospect of bad weather — were likely to be two problems he could well do without and in spite of the cheery expression he assumed for the benefit of his party he was just beginning to have the first misgivings about the whole undertaking. He tried to ascertain from other tour-guides what their plans were. He tried to get a weather-forecast for the next few days. He tried not to notice the occasional build-up of cloud along the horizon which made people frown and reach for their cardigans . . . Please God, he would say silently from time to time looking up into the sky, his heart thumping with anxiety — keep the weather fine — just for two more days. Surely, surely that wasn't too much to ask.

Judith also found herself becoming thoughtful and a little agitated as the end of the holiday drew inevitably near. Like Nikos she was going to have some difficult decisions to make very soon but unlike him, her decisions would affect not only what happened in the next two days but what would happen for the rest of her life. To Peter it all seemed so obvious, so clear-cut. They had found each other again and with Carol's defection to Jeremy — apparently she had decided that, once his tennis-career was over he would make a superb male model! — they were both free, both were at a turning-point in their lives so why not be bold and agree to share whatever the future held.

"Why?" he urged Judith one night when her indecision and pleading with him to stop pressuring her had brought them both close to frustrated tears, " . . . why be miserable apart when we might just as well be miserable together?" causing the threatened tears to dissolve in helpless laughter. That was the trouble. Whenever she tried to be solemn and reasonable and use her common sense Peter would counter her every cautious consideration with some sort of ridiculous practical joke, either burying her in sand, threatening to leave her until she agreed to marry him, pretending to fling himself off a cliff or disappearing under water for what seemed to her far too long for any mortal to survive, only to reappear like a grebe, bobbing up behind her in a splutter of sea-water, dragging her down with him to pretend to drown her instead. He was disarming, charming, fun to be with, really — she had to admit it — he was the only man she ever had or ever could consider marrying. Her problem was not having to decide between Peter and any other man — but whether to choose the married as opposed to the single life. This was proving to be the hardest of all the decisions she had ever had to make in her life before.

"Something will happen to help you decide," Betty reassured her as they stood solemnly in the midst of the Allied Armies' cemetery at Souda Bay, surveying row upon row of neat, white gravestones set in beautifully-kept grounds, "Believe me my dear — there will come a moment when you will *know*." They moved on between the rows, both near to tears in that sad, beautiful place, stopping every now and then to gaze out at the stunning majesty of the bay, where white cotton-wool clouds sailed across the sky, reflected clearly in the tranquil, turquoise sea.

That evening as they assembled on the hotel terrace to drink coffee after their meal at a pizzeria nearby, Nikos addressed his little band of hopefuls while George hung on his every word, not daring to ask if he was to be included, poking sweet, yellow grapes into his mouth rhythmically, automatically like coins into a slot-machine. Judith and Peter sat, hand-in-hand, at the table next to him and Judith could not help stealing an occasional glance at his sweaty, anxious, pudgy face as Nikos outlined the strategy for the next day's adventure. A stiff breeze had sprung up since dusk had fallen and the lanterns hanging from the terrace-roof swung eerily to and fro, casting coloured shadows across all their faces.

"We'll assume it's all systems go," he announced and a little hiss of excitement escaped from his eager yet apprehensive listeners, "but we may yet have to cancel if this wind brings rain by the morning. Now . . . " he deliberately did not look at George but addressed his remarks to the whole group, "you do all appreciate the risks, don't you? Eleven miles of hard slog over rough ground and we have to ford the river several times. Once we are ten minutes into the Gorge there can be no turning back as the bus will have left by then to go over the mountains to Sfakia. Hopefully the boat will be waiting at Roumeli to take us round to meet the bus by sea. I say hopefully as there will only be one boat and it will be the last of the season. So if you cannot make it through the Gorge by four thirty then you could be there all winter if the weather changes suddenly and

you could not get back up the ravine."
They all looked at one another, daring
each other to admit that they suspected
they might not manage after all and
George continued to swallow grapes
and stare unblinkingly at Nikos, daring
him to forbid him to go. There was
a short, significant pause, then Nikos
spoke again.

"Right, folks, we leave at seven a.m.
That will give us time to visit some
of the little chapels along the route
and have a good long rest halfway. Strong shoes, please, comfortable
clothes, water-bottles filled, plasters for
your blisters. Above all, if you worship
any God, pray to Him tonight to send
us good weather tomorrow."

They dispersed, each busy with
their own, anxious thoughts and Peter
clapped a friendly hand on George's
shoulder, muttering a few encouraging
words to him before waylaying Judith as
she was on her way up to bed. Rather
against her will they dropped into the
bar for a last drink. Both were silent as

they contemplated the adventure that lay in store for them next day. At last Peter spoke, his voice serious and his face unusually devoid of his playful, teasing expression.

"Last full day of the holiday tomorrow, Julu," he remarked, turning his head slightly on one side the better to look into her face. She did not reply. She knew what he really meant; not just the end of the holiday but possibly the last chance to snatch at a tempting, delicious dream.

"Yes," she answered, noticing with a slight shock that Peter's abundant, chestnut hair was beginning to be speckled with tiny, sparkling silver points that caught the light as he turned his head again to finish his drink. And he was only nine years older than herself. In nine years time she realised with something of a shock . . . she might be starting to go grey herself.

And nothing to show for it, she thought, as she stared into the mirror an hour later, after setting out everything she needed for the morning in a neat pile on the chair — unless you count a fast car, money in the bank and a pleasant flat of her own. Was that enough? It was more than many people ever achieved, she pondered, more than many people expect to achieve by the time they were forty-nine let alone twenty-nine. She climbed onto the bed and lay with her hands clasped behind her head, frowning and thinking about Peter, about George, about Betty, Brenda and Nikos until they all swirled around her mind as if on a merry-go-round, down and around in a complicated jumble until she thought she'd never get the rest she needed for the challenge that lay ahead.

12

IT was a small party that set out next morning, just ten of them including Nikos, waving self-confidently to Margs, Betty and Carol watching them from the minibus as they began the steep, stony descent into the Gorge. The day had dawned brightly but clouds hovered on the horizon and Nikos intended to set up a smart pace at least until they reached the wide, safe plain beyond the narrowest part of the Gorge known as the Iron Gates where groups had been trapped in the past with occasional fatal results.

In spite of her disturbed night Judith felt fit and alive, keyed up with just enough awareness of danger to make the blood bound through her veins and quicken her heart-beat. She had decided that the problem of Peter and her future could be forgotten for the day so as to channel all her energies into keeping her footing, making sure she did not fall behind and giving a helping hand to George if necessary. The trudge down the stony slope was jarring to the spine but the view as the canyon walls rose higher and higher, casting them all into deep shade as the sky narrowed to a deep-blue, tree-fringed crack was worth a few discomforts along the way. Nikos led the way, trying to keep George with him. Odd to think, mused Judith as she and Peter zigzagged through the pine-woods, skidding slightly on the dusty grit, that his father would last have seen him as a skinny six or seven-year-old. Odd to think that a child can grow older than its parents . . . odd what war and memories of war can do to people.

Could that young soldier — Judith supposed he had only been twenty-seven or eight at the time — running for his life, then dying in this very place have foreseen that, nearly fifty years later, one stout, elderly gentleman would be staggering along, a posy of flowers in his haversack, to pay homage to the puny effort he had made to save the world from the forces of evil? Suddenly she had a nightmare vision of the Gorge as it must have been during those fateful few days in 1941, full of desperately fleeing men, the Germans hot in pursuit — no time then to appreciate the resiny odour of the pine-trees, the pretty red leaves of the maple and the slow circling of buzzards high, high above their heads. It seemed almost obscene for them to be treating this as a day out, a jaunt, little more really than a Sunday School treat — and she had to restrain herself from turning sharply and snapping at Mark and Nigel who were in one of their periodic fits of helpless giggles at some joke that Jeremy had made, the three of them pushing each other about and cackling with mirth. Peter caught sight of her face and narrowed his eyes thoughtfully, slipping a comforting hand briefly into hers.

"Don't blame them — they don't know. No need for us all to be gloomy after all." Judith nodded, sighing and managed a half-hearted smile. She must not be morbid — it was a spectacularly beautiful place, made to be enjoyed. It was not the fault of the place itself that dreadful events had occurred there. But she felt, somewhat soberly, that if Betty had managed to struggle down into those rocky depths she would have been in floods of sympathetic tears by now.

After three hours of non-stop walking the majority of the group reached the deserted village of Samaria, refreshed themselves at the pump and settled down to eat their picnic-lunches. They sat high up in the ruins overlooking the bridge watching all the other groups trailing wearily into the village for their much-needed rest. Nikos really wanted this to be a brief stop in order to get as far down the Gorge as possible — but it was obvious that George, who had been struggling badly, far behind the others for the last hour at least, was going to need a good long rest if he was going to make it through to the end. He'd noticed that Peter and Judith had hovered round him, trying to encourage him to keep up but his weight — and lack of fitness — were beginning to take their toll, as Nikos had feared they would. He lay stretched out on the rocks, his belly a quivering mound, his face almost purple with breathless exhaustion. Nikos allowed him as long as he dared, while party after party passed them by. Then, with an anxious glance up at the thin line of sky above them which had turned from clear blue to ominous grey he urged them all on again. With a chorus of groans and playful threats against Nikos's life they picked themselves up and gathered their possessions from all over the dusty ground. Even in the last few minutes the air had become noticeably cooler.

They were not far now from Ossia Maria, the chapel in which Nikos reckoned it was most likely that George's father had been taken to die. It was the one nearest to the bottom of the Gorge, the most convenient to a crowd of escaping men. It was unlikely that they would have wasted precious time by carrying a badly-injured man very far up the hillside to one of the many other chapels dotted up and down the Gorge.

"Not far now," he encouraged him, giving him a hand to negotiate a particularly bad area of tumbled boulders; and George, his small eyes almost closed against the steady stream of perspiration that poured from his forehead, nodded and grunted in reply, blinking and looking in the direction of Nikos's pointing finger. As they all gazed towards the small, white building almost hidden amongst the trees the sky grew suddenly dark and the whole group raised their heads together like startled deer, alarmed to see a fierce black cloud approaching as a vicious gust of wind blew dust into all their faces. Large blobs of rain, each as big as a marble, first dotted then soaked the boulders — and Judith, watching Nikos's face saw a fleeting expression of panic cross his normally confident face.

She swallowed hard and instinctively moved a little closer to Peter. What was it she had read in Betty's guide-book? That a shower at this time of year could last ten minutes — or ten hours! It could merely serve to lay the dust and freshen up the greenery — or it could turn the quiescent, peaceful area into the bed of a vast, raging torrent that could sweep them all away! The panic-stricken crush that would ensue as all those walkers that had passed them tried to cram through the narrow Iron Gates that still lay ahead of them would be the very worst of all imaginable situations — and to her relief Nikos made the decision she had been hoping he'd make and ordered them all to vacate the path, which was already, after a mere few minutes, turning into a stream and begin to climb the steep side of the ravine, puffing, panting and slithering as they went.

"We'll aim for the chapel," he shouted to them all, "just up there. At least we'll be able to shelter from the rain. Then we'll have to decide what to do." They scrambled obediently after him, the lighthearted banter and joking gone, anxiety rendering each and every one of them silent. Peter called to Mark and between them they heaved the sweating, puffing George up the slope, all three of them stumbling as the stony path became more slippery and dangerous as even quite large stones began to be dislodged by the incessant drumming of the rain.

By the time they reached the chapel and piled inside through the low, cobwebby door, they were all completely drenched through to the skin. Even those who had brought waterproofs with them had not had time to put them on. The chapel had been recently newly-whitewashed and passing walkers had put fresh flowers on the altar — an offertory-box stood underneath one of the tiny windows and those that could reach their purses dropped a few coins in, in gratitude for their shelter from the storm.

They all stood huddled together, the water dripping off their hair and clothes and squelching out of their shoes as they listened in silence to the pitiless drumming of raindrops on the rounded roof and the ever-increasing rustle and gurgle as cascades of rainwater joined to form rivulets, leaping over branches and stones, finding their way along sheep-tracks, running together to form rushing streams, all hastening downhill to swell the ever-deepening, ever-widening river that was, until a few minutes before, their pathway. George's father was forgotten — even by George — as they all pricked their ears to catch that first subtle change in pitch that might herald the end of the rain.

After about a quarter of an hour the sound they had all been waiting for occurred. The drumming of the rain ceased, leaving only the merry gurgle of leaping streams outside the chapel and Nikos emerged gingerly, turning the palms of his hands up to the sky, sniffing the air, a deep, worried frown between his eyes. Had the rain really stopped? Or was this merely a brief interlude between two storms? The frustrating thing was that from here one simply couldn't see enough of the sky to make a reasoned judgement. One had to rely entirely on instinct and experience.

The rain held off . . . and Nikos decided they would take the risk and carry on. It was a gamble — but the alternative, to stay where they were and miss the boat which would then arrive at Chora Sfakion without them to the consternation of Matthiou to say nothing of Betty, Margs and Carol was almost unthinkable. He darted inside the chapel once more and hustled his by now gently-steaming party outside into the air, where they were immediately soaked again by drips falling from the trees.

"Going to have to be a bit of a route-march from now on," he informed them, "no time to pick flowers, compose sonnets or admire the view. Now, have I got everybody? Where on earth is George?"

"He . . . he wants a few quiet minutes in the chapel on his own," explained Peter, rather nervously to Nikos, who reacted with great impatience as Peter had known he would, preparing personally to storm the chapel and drag George out by force. But Peter stopped him, shaking his head.

"It's OK — I'll wait for him, I'll bring him along, I promise. And you're all witnesses to what I'm saying if . . . well, if anything should go wrong it won't be Nikos's fault. No, Judith, you go with the others, I'd far rather you did. Just . . . don't let that boat leave without us — that's all we ask!"

There was really nothing anyone could do. Nikos could not stand there and argue, wasting precious time — he had the rest of the party to worry about. For a moment Judith wavered — if anything should go wrong, Peter had said, his face serious; but nothing could really happen, could it? That was just to put Nikos in the clear — wasn't it? The sky looked brighter now and there was only one way down the Gorge, no chance of their getting lost; and she could quite understand why George should want his quiet moments alone with the memory of his father. Thus comforted, she waved at Peter standing sentinel outside the chapel-door and began to slither after the others on their way back down to the canyon floor.

They made excellent, if muddy, progress for twenty minutes or so, avoiding the torrent that their original pathway had become by edging along the slope just above it, using handy trees to heave themselves along. They were too concerned with simply keeping their footing to be scared and they were actually in sight of the Iron Gates when a tremendous flash of lightning and crack of thunder nearly blinded and deafened them and, in that moment of eerie silence that presages a downpour, Nikos managed to call urgently to his exhausted little flock.

"Run for it — we've got to get through before the rain — everyone run. Come on, come on . . . !" This last exhortation was to Judith who, having glanced behind her every few seconds since they left the chapel, to no avail, stood stock-still, transfixed with sudden horror.

"What about Peter?" she insisted, turning again to try and spot him and George emerging from among the trees, "What about George? We can't go without them — we can't!"

"We must!" replied Nikos and at that moment the heavens opened again and the rain fell relentlessly, straight out of the sky, if anything harder, wetter and in greater quantities than before. Seeing her hesitancy Nikos grabbed Judith's arm, summoning Mark to grasp the other and prepared to hustle her along. Crossly she wrenched her arms away and with her hair plastered over her face and tears mingling with the rain, she made as if to double back up the Gorge to find the missing pair. Nikos was too quick for her and, slithering about on wet stones, managed to block her way. Another flash of lightning lit up the ravine and a crack of thunder, even louder than the first echoed along the cliff corridor, rolling up and down it with great resounding rumbles and Nikos faced Judith with fear and fury in his face.

"Do you want to kill us all?" he shrieked above the noise — and, helplessly, Judith gave way, hating herself for abandoning Peter, covering her face with her hands. Blinded by their straggly hair, rain and blown leaves from the trees, they threw all caution to the winds, risking twisted ankles and broken legs and flung themselves along the boulder-strewn path that was now a fair-sized, fast-flowing river, splashing through water inches deep and rising all the time.

"We've got to get to the Iron Gates before the level rises too high," urged Nikos as one by one the members of his party were forced to rest, gasping, or stumbled over, floundering in the cold, muddy water. "We've got to . . . run, run!"

They ran — even Rosemary forgot her age and ran as if the devil were after her, while Brenda leaped from boulder to boulder, almost succeeding in remaining dry-shod until inevitably she slipped, sprawling full-length in the swirling water. Dennis and Nikos heaved her up between them, hauling her along while the rain poured relentlessly, endlessly down.

By the time they reached the Iron Gates the water, channelled into such a narrow passage was already well over their knees and the force of it actually assisted their passage through. Unable to see where any potholes might be, they simply sloshed through, hoping for the best, Nikos bringing up the rear. Even by the time he had followed everyone through and checked that they had all arrived safely on the other side where the ravine opened out into a wide plain the torrent was reaching a yet higher point on the steep, cliff walls and Judith, her hand to her mouth, stood where Nikos put her, gazing at the gushing force which gained in strength every moment, her eyes round with horror as she thought of the fate in store for Peter and for George.

"They won't be able to get out," she wailed in desperation to Rosemary and Dennis who came and stood with her, their own faces sharp with anxiety as the situation soon became clear to all of them that nobody on the other side of that sheer rocky cleft could hope to get through on foot now without severe danger to their lives.

"He . . . they might be killed," she whispered, sinking down into a crouching position, putting her head on her knees, "People are killed here sometimes," she continued, looking wildly up into Dennis's eyes, "They are, you read about it in the papers — only it's always somebody you don't know . . ."

"Peter won't let himself — or that poor old man — be drowned," reassured Dennis, trying to squeeze muddy water out of his shorts. "He'll sit it out in the chapel — or go back the way we came — or something. Anyway it's almost stopped raining — in a minute he and George'll come popping out of that crack in the rock and we'll all be laughing."

But minutes passed, lengthening into a quarter of an hour, then a half . . . the two of them did not appear, and nobody was laughing. Nikos, his face sharp with anxiety, urged his party on as there was still a good hour's walk ahead of them before they would reach the sea at Roumeli and once more he had difficulty persuading Judith to come along.

"I must know if he's — if they're all right," she kept insisting — but eventually as everyone lost patience with her and began to drift off down the path she was forced to give in and follow them, hating herself for doing so, her mind tortured by what could be happening just a few hundred yards away beyond the Iron Gates.

They could have fallen — been swept away — been knocked out, drowned — anything. She kept saying 'they' but she really meant 'he'. Her concern was all for Peter. He could be dead, he could be dying, he could be in need of a helping hand — and here they all were, walking *away* from him, leaving him to his fate, abandoning him as he had not abandoned George. If he dies, she told herself, tramping automatically in the muddy puddles, simply keeping going without seeing particularly where, I shall blame myself. I *should* have stayed with him at the chapel, we should all have waited . . .

In her heart she knew Nikos had

done the only thing possible in the circumstances — and he had got them all through in more or less reasonable shape. If he had not taken charge in the way he had they might all of them have been drowned instead of just . . . ! Overwhelmed by what she was thinking, trying desperately not to think it, she plodded on mechanically — and at last they reached the sea.

The other parties of walkers that had overtaken them earlier seemed surprised to see how wet they were and clustered round, anxious to hear their story. The sun came out strongly as if to tease them and very soon rows of colourful clothing were spread out along the terraces of the little cafés while their owners, down to their undies, sunbathed or chatted together in low, worried tones, while they waited for the boat to Chora Sfakion to arrive. Judith sat apart, her clothes drying on her, encasing her in dry mud, her face a pale mask of misery as the hours passed agonisingly slowly by.

At last the boat was spotted, an old blue steamer that looked as if it had seen better days and as soon as it had drawn up alongside the rickety pier there was a stampede to get on. Nikos had tried to put a phone-call through to the police at Chania to report his two missing persons but the storm had interfered with the telephone-wires and he could not get a connection. However encouragingly he had to act in front of Judith and the rest of the party he could not deny to himself that he was extremely anxious and growing more so by the minute. Suppose . . . just suppose, as Judith feared, they *were* dead. It was possible — every tour-guide knew only too well that it was possible. How could he face her or any of his group, his family, his friends, the press . . . how could he carry on after a tragedy such as that?

He pulled himself together, ushering his party onto the boat, where they all collapsed in varying stages of exhaustion, too tired even to stagger to the coffee-bar to buy drinks. Judith remained stubbornly on the beach facing that gap in the trees by the café where the path from the Gorge appeared, staring and staring, silent and motionless — and he approached her gently, sitting down beside her, hardly able to bear to see the look in her eyes.

"The boatman has agreed to wait another half-hour," he told her quietly, "after that he has to go as it will get dark very soon. Why not get on the boat — you can watch for them just as well from there?"

But she would not be moved. There would be people on the boat telling her not to worry, not to be silly, trying to comfort her when there could be no comforting. She stayed sitting on the beach, bolt upright, outwardly calm, her mind settled into an unshakeable resolve. "Something will happen to help you decide," Betty had said to her as they looked at the graves at Souda Bay, "you will *know*." Something *had* happened — perhaps something too awful to contemplate and her decision was going to come too late. But nothing she had ever experienced could match these frightful hours for anxiety, misery and horror — if Peter *should* survive, she was never going to let him out of her sight again for a single minute of her life!

She waited — and waited. The boatman rang his bell once, twice. Nikos came out to remonstrate with her twice, three times. But still she did not move. Then, just as she began to notice the shadows lengthen and a little chill crept into the early evening air, her eyes, aching from the strain of looking began to play her tricks. She thought she saw two figures wavering and wobbling in her view, growing larger, a little steadier, then — unbelievably — recognisable as they stumbled out of the trees and across the sandy beach towards the boat, waving frantically at the boatman who was already beginning his preparations for casting off. Hardly anyone on board was sufficiently awake to see Judith rise unsteadily to her feet and stumble over towards the tall, chestnut-haired man, his clothes soaked in water, mud, sticks, leaves and sandy grit and lean helplessly against his sopping, dirty chest. They clung together, rocking slightly from side to side — and the boatman rang his bell again, loudly and insistently, disturbing all his indignant and weary passengers who, wondering what the crisis was, jerked awake one by one. Then on catching sight first of George, then of Peter and Judith, oblivious to the world, they catcalled and cheered, clapping, applauding as the two of them kissed and kissed again.

"You gave me the most dreadful fright," sobbed Judith, hitting at Peter's strong, mud-spattered arms, looking at him with fiery fury in her eyes. "Don't you dare, *dare* ever do that again!" He held her tightly, calming her, stroking her streaked, stiff hair, sharing her tears; until Nikos, pale and sweating with relief jumped off the boat for the fourth time to greet both him and George, hugging them both in an ecstasy of joy, whilst urging them as tactfully as possible off the stony beach and towards the old blue boat.

13

"YOU mean, you *swam* through the Iron Gates?"

In spite of their leg-weariness, hunger and general exhaustion, all the members of their own party — and others — clustered round Peter and George as the steamer got under way, the engine working full-blast to try to make up lost time. Nobody had eyes for the golden loveliness of the Libyan Sea, each ripple touched with the glow of late-afternoon sunshine. The attention was all on the two mud-soaked, weary heroes who lay sprawled on the deck, too tired even to raise their heads to drink the cups of tea and coffee with which they were generously and continuously plied.

"No choice — we had to," Peter tried to explain, his hand clasped tight by Judith who sat beside him, her eyes never leaving his face. As he spoke, flakes of drying mud fell from his forehead and around his mouth and Judith brushed them away with trembling fingers. "We hadn't any idea how deep the water was . . . couldn't see the bottom! And when you've never seen the place before you can't tell what the level should be." He stopped a moment, frowning as if remembering and looked over towards George who had fallen asleep and was snoring noisily, his mouth wide open, on the other side of the deck.

"It got pretty deep as we were approaching the Iron Gates — then George slipped and I really thought he was gone, the force of the water was so great! No hope of getting him out so I took a gamble and simply let myself go too. Really then the water did the rest, taking us through the gap like a couple of canoes shooting the rapids." He half-smiled at the memory and looked mischievously up into Judith's scared, blue eyes. "I think between us we've invented a new sport, George and I. Copped a few bruises along the way — but, looking back, it was really quite good fun."

His voice tailed away as he felt tears dropping on to his face and, instantly solemn, he put up a hand and stroked Judith's dirty, worried face.

"It wasn't fun for us," he heard her murmur, "I thought you were dead — both of you. And there was absolutely nothing I could do . . . " Her voice shook as she relived those ghastly hours when her imagination had conjured up vision after vision of Peter's drowned, broken, battered body before her eyes. Peter looked at her through a haze of weariness and attempted a cautious, tender smile. He squeezed her hand as tightly as he could, pulling her slightly towards him. All around them people were nodding off, swaying and slipping awkwardly off their seats as utter weariness overtook them. For a long moment they held each other's gaze; then the skin around Peter's eyes and mouth wrinkled into crow's feet and he spoke lightly, his voice only just audible above the rumble and roar of the tough little engine below them.

"I was thinking of asking you to marry me," he remarked casually, as if the thought had only that moment occurred to him. His gaze roved over her matted hair, streaked muddy face and still damply-steaming and very smelly clothes, "only I'm not at all sure if I'd like to live with such a very dirty wife."

This remark, coming from a man not only caked in mud from head to toe with dead leaves and wet grass in his hair, but also with a strong aroma of decaying weed, murky river-water and wet leather about him was too much for Judith to resist and she collapsed in helpless laughter, the relief at seeing him alive, well and able to crack jokes almost too much for her composure.

"Well," she replied, laughter struggling with tears, pretending to consider the subject seriously, "I suppose I could think about it — but I'm not at all sure I could live with such a very wet and muddy man."

"Come here," he replied, his voice gruffly thick, pulling her closely to him, staring solemnly into her red-rimmed, tear-filled eyes, "are we or are we not engaged?" he asked her, the urgent appeal in his eyes belying the frivolous tone of his voice — and after a final moment of hesitancy, she nodded firmly, frowning to stop herself from weeping and glanced round at the sprawled and sleeping passengers scattered round the boat.

"We are engaged," she agreed and — in the absence of any conscious witnesses, were able to seal their bond with a kiss so long and hard that Judith wondered briefly if she would ever be able to breathe normally again. Utter weariness, coupled with a deep flood of happiness, overwhelmed them both and, unable to lift a toe or finger, the two of them slid together into an ungainly, grubby heap on the deck, their arms tightly around each other. To the thud of the engine and the regular slap of the waves, with the last of the sun glowing golden on their faces and a warm breeze to wrap them round they sank into a well-deserved, contented and exhausted sleep.

* * *

Later — much later — that night Judith sighed and stirred in Peter's encircling arms.

Soon it would be time to say goodbye. To young Brenda, still starry-eyed with desire for the unattainable Nikos, to Rosemary and Dennis, to Mark and Nigel, to George, his fifty-year quest accomplished. It would be a sad good-bye to Betty and Margs, that indomitable couple, already planning to save up for another five years to visit Egypt before either of them died and a strange one to Jeremy and Carol who seemed to have all the makings of an excellent partnership. And to

Nikos himself, of course, who had presided over problems, alarms, fights and emergencies with commendable sang-froid and could now settle down to the comparative calm and tranquillity of the winter season.

But there would be no good-bye to Peter — not this time. From the moment they stumbled off the boat and onto the minibus where the story of Peter's and George's narrow escape was told and re-told in more and more graphic detail to Betty, Margs and Carol, they had not let each other out of sight. That steaming hot bath back at the hotel, though a little crowded with two, after their experiences in the Gorge, was one of the most delicious sensations Judith could recall as the mud and dirt fell from their aching bodies and out of their hair, colouring the water to a rich, gritty brown — so that they needed a second bath immediately after the first. Then there was the farewell supper at which the story of the flood had to be told again and again and at which almost everyone had fallen unashamedly asleep. Now here they were, she and Peter, together for the last night of the holiday — and for the rest of their lives. In spite of her exhaustion Judith woke several times during the night to gloat again and again over her good fortune, silently blessing the fates that had arranged for herself and Peter to meet again after so many years apart.

Not everyone gets a second chance, she'd mused, propping herself up on her elbows the better to study Peter's moonlit, sleeping face . . . and this chance had been so nearly lost. She'd snuggled down again in deep contentment, sure now where her future lay — and wondered idly what her career-crazy friends in London would say when they heard she'd swopped life in the fast lane for marriage, country life and babies. She chuckled in the darkness — at least, living in the wilds of Somerset, she would not have to face them every day and be forced to keep explaining and justifying her change of heart.

Peter must have been thinking along the same lines . . . as he struggled momentarily out of sleep and looked, at first surprised, and then delighted to see Judith beside him. He frowned a little, pursing up his lips.

"What's the matter?" asked Judith, almost drowned by drowsiness as she felt his strong arms about her and his warm breath on her brow as he stared into her face.

"There's something we've been forgetting," he uttered — and Judith frowned too, puzzled by his almost comical look of concern; and he continued, "I mean, this hateful creature who has dared to put in an offer for our house. We've got to find a way to get rid of him even if we have to resort to bribery and corruption." Judith relaxed, flopping back onto the bed and laughed and laughed again, while Peter fumed with curiosity and pretended rage.

"It's OK," she managed to jerk out at last when she paused to take a breath, "I was going to tell you — sometime, only the right opportunity never seemed to come up. That offer — you don't have to worry, Peter. Stella would have asked far too many nosey questions and jumped to far too many conclusions if I'd told her a friend wanted the place. So, on her recommendation, I put in that offer myself. I suppose I might just let you go halves, though . . . "

She had no chance to explain further as Peter rolled her over, threatening to tip her out of bed, unable to do more than splutter with delighted surprise. They would be tired tomorrow — they were tired now. But with so much to celebrate, so many plans to make, so much to say to each other that simply could not wait until the morning they could hardly be blamed for laughing and loving the night away.

WITH SOMEBODY ELSE
Theresa Charles

Rosamond sets off for Cornwall with Hugo to meet his family, blissfully unaware of the shocks in store for her.

A SUMMER FOR STRANGERS
Claire Hamilton

Because she had lost her job, her flat and she had no money, Tabitha agreed to pose as Adam's future wife although she believed the scheme to be deceitful and cruel.

VILLA OF SINGING WATER
Angela Petron

The disquieting incidents that occurred at the Vatican and the Colosseum did not trouble Jan at first, but then they became increasingly unpleasant and alarming.

DOCTOR NAPIER'S NURSE
Pauline Ash

When cousins Midge and Derry are entered as probationer nurses on the same day but at different hospitals they agree to exchange identities.

A GIRL LIKE JULIE
Louise Ellis

Caroline absolutely adored Hugh Barrington, but then Julie Crane came into their lives. Julie was the kind of girl who attracts men without even trying.

COUNTRY DOCTOR
Paula Lindsay

When Evan Richmond bought a practice in a remote country village he did not realise that a casual encounter would lead to the loss of his heart.

ENCORE
Helga Moray

Craig and Janet realise that their true happiness lies with each other, but it is only under traumatic circumstances that they can be reunited.

NICOLETTE
Ivy Preston

When Grant Alston came back into her life, Nicolette was faced with a dilemma. Should she follow the path of duty or the path of love?

THE GOLDEN PUMA
Margaret Way

Catherine's time was spent looking after her father's Queensland farm. But what life was there without David, who wasn't interested in her?

HOSPITAL BY THE LAKE
Anne Durham

Nurse Marguerite Ingleby was always ready to become personally involved with her patients, to the despair of Brian Field, the Senior Surgical Registrar, who loved her.

VALLEY OF CONFLICT
David Farrell

Isolated in a hostel in the French Alps, Ann Russell sees her fiancé being seduced by a young girl. Then comes the avalanche that imperils their lives.

NURSE'S CHOICE
Peggy Gaddis

A proposal of marriage from the incredibly handsome and wealthy Reagan was enough to upset any girl — and Brooke Martin was no exception.

A DANGEROUS MAN
Anne Goring

Photographer Polly Burton was on safari in Mombasa when she met enigmatic Leon Hammond. But unpredictability was the name of the game where Leon was concerned.

PRECIOUS INHERITANCE
Joan Moules

Karen's new life working for an authoress took her from Sussex to a foreign airstrip and a kidnapping; to a real life adventure as gripping as any in the books she typed.

VISION OF LOVE
Grace Richmond

When Kathy takes over the rundown country kennels she finds Alec Stinton, a local vet, very helpful. But their friendship arouses bitter jealousy and a tragedy seems inevitable.

CRUSADING NURSE
Jane Converse

It was handsome Dr. Corbett who opened Nurse Susan Leighton's eyes and who set her off on a lonely crusade against some powerful enemies and a shattering struggle against the man she loved.

WILD ENCHANTMENT
Christina Green

Rowan's agreeable new boss had a dream of creating a famous perfume using her precious Silverstar, but Rowan's plans were very different.

DESERT ROMANCE
Irene Ord

Sally agrees to take her sister Pam's place as La Chartreuse the dancer, but she finds out there is more to it than dyeing her hair red and looking like her sister.

HEART OF ICE
Marie Sidney

How was January to know that not only would the warmth of the Swiss people thaw out her frozen heart, but that she too would play her part in helping someone to live again?

LUCKY IN LOVE
Margaret Wood

Companion-secretary to wealthy gambler Laura Duxford, who lived in Monaco, seemed to Melanie a fabulous job. Especially as Melanie had already lost her heart to Laura's son, Julian.

NURSE TO PRINCESS JASMINE
Lilian Woodward

Nick's surgeon brother, Tom, performs an operation on an Arabian princess, and she invites Tom, Nick and his fiancé to Omander, where a web of deceit and intrigue closes about them.

THE WAYWARD HEART
Eileen Barry

Disaster-prone Katherine's nickname was "Kate Calamity", but her boss went too far with an outrageous proposal, which because of her latest disaster, she could not refuse.

FOUR WEEKS IN WINTER
Jane Donnelly

Tessa wasn't looking forward to meeting Paul Mellor again — she had made a fool of herself over him once before. But was Orme Jared's solution to her problem likely to be the right one?

SURGERY BY THE SEA
Sheila Douglas

Medical student Meg hadn't really wanted to go and work with a G.P. on the Welsh coast although the job had its compensations. But Owen Roberts was certainly not one of them!

HEAVEN IS HIGH
Anne Hampson

The new heir to the Manor of Marbeck had been found. But it was rather unfortunate that when he arrived unexpectedly he found an uninvited guest, complete with stetson and high boots.

LOVE WILL COME
Sarah Devon

June Baker's boss was not really her idea of her ideal man, but when she went from third typist to boss's secretary overnight she began to change her mind.

ESCAPE TO ROMANCE
Kay Winchester

Oliver and Jean first met on Swale Island. They were both trying to begin their lives afresh, but neither had bargained for complications from the past.

CASTLE IN THE SUN
Cora Mayne

Emma's invalid sister, Kym, needed a warm climate, and Emma jumped at the chance of a job on a Mediterranean island. But Emma soon finds that intrigues and hazards lurk on the sunlit isle.

BEWARE OF LOVE
Kay Winchester

Carol Brampton resumes her nursing career when her family is killed in a car accident. With Dr. Patrick Farrell she begins to pick up the pieces of her life, but is bitterly hurt when insinuations are made about her to Patrick.

DARLING REBEL
Sarah Devon

When Jason Farradale's secretary met with an accident, her glamorous stand-in was quite unable to deal with one problem in particular.

THE PRICE OF PARADISE
Jane Arbor

It was a shock to Fern to meet her estranged husband on an island in the middle of the Indian Ocean, but to discover that her father had engineered it puzzled Fern. What did he hope to achieve?

DOCTOR IN PLASTER
Lisa Cooper

When Dr. Scott Sutcliffe is injured, Nurse Caroline Hurst has to cope with a very demanding private case. But when she realises her exasperating patient has stolen her heart, how can Caroline possibly stay?

A TOUCH OF HONEY
Lucy Gillen

Before she took the job as secretary to author Robert Dean, Cadie had heard how charming he was, but that wasn't her first impression at all.

ROMANTIC LEGACY
Cora Mayne

As kennelmaid to the Armstrongs, Ann Brown, had no idea that she would become the central figure in a web of mystery and intrigue.

THE RELENTLESS TIDE
Jill Murray

Steve Palmer shared Nurse Marie Blane's love of the sea and small boats. Marie's other passion was her step-brother. But when danger threatened who should she turn to — her step-brother or the man who stirred emotions in her heart?

ROMANCE IN NORWAY
Cora Mayne

Nancy Crawford hopes that her visit to Norway will help her to start life again. She certainly finds many surprises there, including unexpected happiness.

UNLOCK MY HEART
Honor Vincent

When Ruth Linton, a young widow with three children, inherits a house in the country, it seems to be the answer to her dreams. But Ruth's problems were only just beginning . . .

SWEET PROMISE
Janet Dailey

Erica had met Rafael in Mexico, where their relationship had been brief but dramatic. Now, over a year later in Texas, she had met him again — and he had the power to wreck her life.

SAFARI ENCOUNTER
Rosemary Carter

Jenny had to accept that she couldn't run her father's game park alone; so she let forceful Joshua Adams virtually take over. But Joshua took over her heart as well!